BEHIND THE LINES

Behind the Lines

by

IDALIS WOOD

Adelaide Books
New York / Lisbon
2019

BEHIND THE LINES
By Idalis Wood

Copyright © by Idalis Wood
Cover design © 2019 Adelaide Books

Published by Adelaide Books, New York / Lisbon
adelaidebooks.org
Editor-in-Chief
Stevan V. Nikolic

For any information, please address Adelaide Books
at info@adelaidebooks.org
or write to:
Adelaide Books
244 Fifth Ave. Suite D27
New York, NY, 10001

ISBN: 978-1-951896-03-4
Printed in the United States of America

Contents

I.

Foot in the Sand

It was the third year, seventh month, and second week of Lila's job as a personal assistant and copy editor to Johnson Walker of Foot in the Sand Publishing in New York. From getting coffee to proofreading manuscripts, Lila took on more work than her job description required all in the hopes that it would be the day where Walker would promote her. He didn't ask her to bring him coffee or lunch in nearly six months. Lila's hopes were high. After three spurned manuscripts, two stories accepted for the next issue, and five meetings scheduled for the upcoming week, she became less optimistic.

"You've got to look for a better job, *chica*! I mean, how much longer will you lay around and stick with bland compromise?" asked Jay. She was Lila's engaged soon-to-be former roommate. Her tone was more sharp and intense this time.

"It pays the rent." A prepared comeback with no more staying power.

"Just look for something else. You shouldn't be stuck in one job to the point of resenting it, *amiga. Negación no es sólo un río.*"

Lila hated it when Jay spoke Spanish to her for the reason she knew that Jay knew she won the argument. Everything sounded powerful in Spanish.

Jay rolled her eyes, and prepared for a new topic. "I have almost everything I need for the something borrowed and all, but I need something old."

"What about your *abuela's* veil?"

Jay pondered. "If I can find it."

During the ride back to the apartment, Lila stared out of the window of the bus, the streetlights becoming blurs and the cluster of boarding houses hidden in the shadows. Inside the bus, Lila stood out from the other passengers; smartly dressed in a pencil skirt, vintage-style blouse, and heather gray heels. Everyone else wore pants with an elastic waist paired with graphic T-shirts. Their feet were either covered by a myriad of sneakers or flip-flops revealing feet in need of fifty-dollar pedicures. No one paid much attention to Lila or to anyone else unless they were blocked from their designated exits.

It was once Lila was inside her Brooklyn apartment where she could dress in comfort. Her pajamas, flannel with Hello Kitty shorts, released her from her need to be an adult. She wore her fluffy socks with all of her five feet and one inch pride, until she needed a step stool to reach the cereal in the cabinet. *Very funny, Jay.*

Back at Foot in the Sand, Lila was welcomed with a stack of manuscripts that needing to be edited. Most were more than fifty pages. Lila skipped her lunch hour to be able to leave early. Snacking on grapes and kettle chips, Lila looked up to see Johnson Walker heading in her direction. The stern look on his weathered face indicated either Lila looked over a mistake or she wasn't working fast enough in his eyes. It was the latter.

"We're going to be behind if you don't get these done," Walker reminded Lila coldly, pressing on the somewhat smaller sized stack of manuscripts firmly with his index finer—the ones she completed.

This is beyond my job description. "I'll stay in late or take what I don't have finished home with me if I have to," responded Lila as courteous as she could manage.

"Good." Walker marched off and barricaded himself in the spacious office overlooked the city.

By six 'o' clock, Lila managed to finish the last of the manuscripts and delivered them to Walker's office. With a gruff exhale, Walker sent Lila on her way. It was the first time Lila had been eager to leave. Her black high heels clicked on the tiled floor as they pinched her toes; Lila was the last to leave. She texted Jay about wanting to join her for drinks. Jay was all too eager.

"Are you going to listen to me now, *mija*?" she asked Lila after the first round of cocktails.

"I've been contemplating what to add on my résumé," answered Lila. "How do I say 'worked in the same position for almost five years far above my skill set while less qualified assholes moved up' in a professional way?"

Jay nearly spat out her Cosmopolitan. "I take it you don't want Walks-All-Over-You as a reference?"

"Well, fuck."

"Want me to make the conversation more light?"

Lila nodded.

"Debating whether or not to go with a mermaid style dress or A-line. Opinions?"

"Go A-line. It'll give you more room if you want to dance. Did you find the veil, yet?"

Jay shook her head. "I'll miss hanging out with you."

"Same." *Who will tell me gossip and not judge me for going to that cheap Chinese food truck down the street?* "It'll be so odd with the place so quiet." *If you don't count the occasional police siren and local arguments.*

"You'll manage."

"Goods, in my office now," barked Walker in a low, serious tone.

Lila was out of her cubicle instantly. The high ceiling of the office made her feel small and mousy, hiding the looks of mock concern form her other colleagues. "What is it, Mr. Walker?"

"Did you or did you not approve a woman's manuscript of people's encounters with guardian angels?" he asked, his eyes like cold daggers.

Lila nodded, her eyes darting between Walker's and her boots.

"I see." Walker pressed the tips of his fingers together. "And you did this deed *without* any consulting or approval from me?"

"Yes," Lila peeped.

"I see." Walker got up from his desk, strolling toward Lila. "And why, might I include in asking, did you such a thing without my knowledge, let alone my approval?"

"I, um—"

"Um is not an answer."

Walker leaned back onto his desk.

Lila cleared her throat. "The manuscript needed minimal editing…when I was done, you were busy, so I sent it to our conglomerate because Joey said they needed something quick."

"Ah! And you were ready and willing to send over a piece when you don't have the experience, yet. Whether or not you knew that this would come back to me, which I know you know." Walker continued his air of mock revelation.

"I…I have experience… I ran my college newspaper and have had stories published at least three separate times—"

Walker held up his hand, stopping Lila. "I'm aware. No need to reiterate your résumé. I hired you as a copy editor. That's all you're capable of being."

Lila's eyes grew wide. "Excuse me?"

"I haven't seen you try to move up from it. Unless you don't want to be anything more than a proofreader, tell me now or this meeting is over."

"I want to be a commissioning editor."

Walker seemed pleased. "Well, you have the gumption to be one, as our conglomerate approved your manuscript. It appears you know what we represent."

Lila smiled, but knew something else was coming.

"Remembering your résumé, you have the necessary degree in English Literature. Unfortunately, you seem to lack any administrative knowledge."

Excuse me? "I took three business courses at Sarah Lawrence."

Walker smiled. "I like you wanting more in this job."

"So..?" Lila leaned forward.

"Not yet."

Lila's hopes were broken.

"I need you to prove you're dedicated to this new job, and who knows, I might make you Editor In-Chief if you prove yourself." Walker headed back to his desk.

"How do I do that?"

"You will shadow me starting next Monday to get a handle of the administration side of things during my visit to one of our conglomerates in Brooklyn. Be packed and here at 7:30 AM. Sharp." Walker shooed Lila back to her designated cubicle.

During the lunch break, Lila made her way down 5th Avenue from 15th Street to her favorite hot dog vendor between a Chase Bank and Wedgwood House for a foot long with the works. Johnny, the South-African middle-aged man, greeted Lila warmly and presented her with her lunch before she could get her wallet out.

"I got chance to prove myself to be Editor In-Chief," said Lila, handing Johnny a five and taking momentary shade under one of the vendor's blue umbrellas.

"Has he given you any clue as to how you are going to do that? An assignment?" Johnny pressed.

"I'm shadowing him next Monday in Manhattan."

Johnny raised his eyebrows, handing Lila her change. "Aren't you better than that?"

"If this is one of the steps I have to take, then what's the harm in it?"

"If you are already good at your job, you would've been promoted already."

The melody of taxicabs, cyclists, and honking horns filled the air as Lila trekked her way back to Foot in the Sand. Passing all of the steel and glass buildings and shop windows brought attention to Lila's still uncomfortable high heels and her fairly modest, corporate attire. She looked like she belonged. Heading back into the publishing office, there was a construction site of a new Starbucks.

What the hell did Johnny mean when he said I'm better than shadowing Walker? Does he want me to stay in this position for the rest of my life? Lila demanded internally, biting into the last bit of her hot dog angrily. *I have the chance to do more with my life! Show my mom and dad I can achieve success like oh-so-perfect Camille.*

"Congratulations on your win!" cheered her mom, hugging then fourteen-year-old sister Camille with my dad.

At ten years old, I was the photographer. I took the picture of them with Cammy holding her first place art piece, a watercolor rendition of Salvador Dali's The Persistence of Memory. *Original.*

"This is going in a frame!" Dad stated as I handed the camera back.

I won second place at the poetry recital the day before, but it didn't matter.

"You're going to be a famous artist one day, and as your parents, we'll be keeping this original. It'll be priceless," added Mom as we headed back to the car.

Back home, there were more photos of Camille and her accomplishments. Most of my achievements were certificates of excellence and academic standing whereas Camille's involved her photo paired with trophies. Each one showed Camille growing more beautiful as time passed; curves becoming more pronounced and feminine, light touches of makeup making her alabaster skin glow, and her nightfall hair once confined in pigtails now a sleek ponytail or braid. My photos were kept in the privacy of yearbooks; an adorable girl with her front teeth missing to a pre-teen with small spots of acne and a bobbed haircut and unflattering bangs.

Cammy was and still remains Daphne. I'm still Velma.

Monday was as mundane as they came. Sharing a taxi with Walker intimidated Lila. She had her own car, a 2005 Honda Civic, but Walker insisted on her riding with him. Even sitting down, Lila felt small. No amount of uncomfortable heels disguised her 5'1" frame. The top of his head a few inches from the roof of the taxi cab. Driving on the Brooklyn Bridge felt as if both Walker and Lila had entered a brand new world. When the two reached Brooklyn, there was the same essence of exhaust fumes and dust from construction both were familiar with.

After Walker paid for the taxi, he led Lila inside Melville House. The interior consisted of stark white walls and gleaming, ceiling high windows. Each window was divided into 4x6 sections, adorning the hardwood floor with a checkerboard shadow when the sun appeared. On the display shelves, neatly stacked piles of books were placed according to genre, author, and the most eye-catching cover design. A man in his early thirties dressed in slacks and a blue pressed button down shirt greeted Walker and Lila formally and cordially.

"You brought a negotiator?" the man joked, facing Walker and addressing Lila. "You don't seem like the type to ask for a second opinion."

"Like I need one," Walker chided out of earshot from Lila, who was standing beside him.

"I'm sure. And your name?" He turned to face Lila.

She was surprised at his firm grip. "Lila Goods."

"Lincoln Barns." The man turned to address Walker again. "What brings her in?"

"She's in line for the head editor position back at FTS, and I need her to get some administrative experience."

"Any suggestions?"

"I'm thinking about having her do some bookkeeping, inventory of what's being shipped, and corresponding with other branches of the company."

"Sounds good."

Lincoln turned to address Lila. "How long do you expect to be here?"

Lila shrugged her shoulders. "I wasn't given an approximate length of stay, but I'm open for however long it will take me to require the necessary experience."

"I like her, Johnson. Why didn't you send her here sooner?"

"I keep her busy." Walker's response was too quick.

"What's my first task?" Lila chirped.

"The house is expecting a shipment from Sterling in a few minutes. I'll lead you to the desk for you to sign the package and consult with their leading man."

"Yes, sir."

"Nice seeing you again, Johnson. Hope you send more lovelies my way." With a quick handshake, Walker left Melville House Publishing. He looked back to see Lila being lead to a separate room with an official desk with an iMac desktop computer, sleek wireless mouse, small stack of files, work phone, and blank nameplate.

"The files here are orders we have on back order at the moment. Textbook season is in the air, and many don't really want to pay through their school," explained Lincoln. "Some of them have come in, and I'll need you to find them from what we have in stock. I'll have someone come help you so you can see to the delivery early and consult with the head from Sterling."

"What time will he be arriving, sir?" inquired Lila.

"Call me Link. I'm not that old, yet, and by my accounts there isn't an age gap between us."

"Maybe six years." Lila blushed slightly.

"26?"

Lila nodded.

"Not bad, Lila. And he arrives at 1:30." Walker glanced at his watch. "It's 10:30; should give you time to get some lunch. Dial 307, and it'll connect you to the Chinese place down the block. They'll be open in a few minutes."

"Oh. I, um, brought a PB and J for lunch. It's got to be in here somewhere…" She fished it out of her purse, producing a flattened and misshapen lunch in a Ziploc bag. Lincoln was all too quick to snatch it away and discard it in a nearby wastebasket.

"You're not ten, Lila. I'll get Greta to help you with the back orders and I'll call Golden Dragon for a sample platter. You get a half hour lunch and ten minute warning for any meetings and consultants."

Lincoln's manner of professionalism and candid concern warmed Lila's heart. Had her position not been temporary and if she met Lincoln outside of the workplace, she'd attempt to seek his attention for the prize of an awkward dinner and drinks. She'd wear her favorite red dress, a slash of lipstick, and wait at the bar for Lincoln to come to her first. After all, red is the color most associated with passion and arousal for men. Clearly something that didn't make her look "adorable." Clearly he was no different, but there was something else about Lincoln diverging with Lila's assumptions. He was fairly young, kind, and open. He was the opposite of Walker; pleasant, spirited, authoritative without being intimidating, and Lincoln's blue eyes and clean-cut features only enhanced his friendliness. He looked like someone Camille could catch with just a flip of her raven hair and flutter of her lashes, but his attention was on Lila; an act that was both welcoming and unfamiliar to her. While he might not have been looking at her the way others looked at Camille, Lila settled on Lincoln looking at her with respect. She might as well enjoy it for however long she was permitted to stay.

Meanwhile, Lila's helper Greta was a dark-skinned, stern-looking, but welcoming single mother with a young daughter. She went to art school in California, leaving to be closer to her family upon graduation. Until Lincoln's father hired her as an editorial photographer and medical illustrator, Greta formerly worked as a caricature artist and graphic designer.

"Glad he gave me a chance," she said. "Beats being forty years old and living with my parents."

"How long have you been here?" Lila asked, preparing the latest shipment of back ordered books.

"About ten years. I've been here back when Link's dad ran the place. When he died, Link got the business and a strict guideline on how the place was to be run," Greta informed. "I like my job, and I provide a nice life for me and my daughter. She's been in a few shoots for Gap Kids since we've lived here, but she's not touching the money until she's eighteen."

"Seems like your daughter is famous."

"Irene is well-known; not famous." Greta placed a pen in the center of her tight, black bun. "You get back to your post and Link know Stevie know to get these shipped."

"Stevie?"

"His parents actually named him that."

As she sat down at her desk, Lila was greeted with a phone call from Sterling Publishing. The man's voice on the other line was dry and direct. "Yes, I'm calling to confirm a 1:30 meeting with Mr. Barn's consultant."

Lila looked at her computer monitor for a brief moment, noticing the meeting reminder on the calendar icon. "Your meeting has been confirmed, and may I ask for a name to give to Lin—Mr. Barns?"

"Arthur Samson."

The call ended. Lila wrote the name on a Post It note, and then pressed the button with the label "Lincoln."

"You can come into my office, you know?" he said, hanging up.

Frustrated by another abrupt and borderline rude phone conversation, Lila strolled into Lincoln's office. The door was open to reveal an office with a small window and pictures of Lincoln with two small children and woman whom Lila assumed was his wife, a gorgeously framed diploma and degrees from Cornell University, and a certificate of excellence for humanitarian work. He was too good for Lila, but perfect for Camille if he were single.

"You're home early," Mom said. I was home before 8:30 PM. "What did you two do?"

"He wanted to take me to a train show. He just spent the entire time talking about trains to the point where I couldn't get a word in."

"Jeopardy" was on.

Before I could complain further, Camille came home from her date. She was pink in the cheeks and smiling a mile wide.

"How did I get so lucky to find him?" she cooed.

I left the living room to watch TV in the comfort of my room as Mom predictably gravitated to the happier and love-struck daughter. During commercials, I overheard the mother and daughter conversing about Camille's date talking her on a walk in the park, a picnic, and a dance under the stars to a mix tape he made.

From then on, I decided she'd never listen in on Camille's dating life while deciding not to go on anymore dates Mom set up with those Camille rejected previously.

I'm no one's Cousin Oliver.

"Have you and Greta finished processing the back orders?" Lincoln probed, looking up from his computer.

"Yes, and Stevie just shipped them," Lila answered.

"Excellent. Is the appointment still on?"

"Yes. I just confirmed it, and Sterling is sending a Arthur Samson to negotiate."

Lincoln sucked air between his teeth in trepidation. "They're playing hardball. Great." He rose from his seat. His stature didn't intimidate Lila despite Lincoln being about the same height as Walker. Lincoln's physique was more average, as opposed to Walker who still held remnants of being a star athlete in his peak. "I better be with you when Samson comes in."

"What are you going to do? Are you handling negotiations? What's your plan?"

"*You're* handling the negotiations, Lila. He's meeting you, not me. I'll be there to help you navigate. Samson's known for trying to get the minimum for getting the work published and circulated."

"Should we discuss tactics? Come up with a game plan?" Lila held a clipboard to her chest.

"Good idea. We'll discuss it during lunch." Lincoln's phone rang. "Hello? Send him in. Thanks."

After a filling lunch of pork fried rice and wontons, Lila felt she was informed enough and ready to face Sterling Publishing's negotiator. As Lincoln previously stated, he would be there to oversee her without intervening unless Lila expressed a need for his assistance.

The moment the overhead clock read 1:30 PM, the front doors of Melville opened to a colossus of a man in a black pinstripe suit. He immediately fixed his eyes on Lincoln and suppressed a smirk when he sniffed out the timid Lila. She understood how Arthur Samson, the man coming toward her and Lincoln, would be Sterling's "Mad Dog." His shoulders were wide, his stance confident, and his gray-blue eyes could pierce though the soul of the most hardened criminal. His thin lips pressed into so tight a line made Lila assume he wasn't one who cracked jokes with his friends. If he had any.

"Mr. Barns," Arthur Samson greeted, his low and hoarse.

"Mr. Samson. Come with us," Lincoln returned, addressing Lila.

"Who's this?" Samson peered down at Lila.

"We spoke on the phone, sir. Lila Goods." Lila forced herself to stay polite. "I'm the consultant you'll be speaking with this afternoon."

Arthur smiled. Lila was familiar with it: the "how cute" smile. "How long have you been here, honey?"

Lila resisted the urge to roll her eyes. "Mr. Barns has briefed me. I'm certain we can come to an agreement about the logistics of the next book shipment and publishing details."

Lincoln smiled and led the way to his office. "We're prepared to offer a maximum of four hundred for the manuscript. Six hundred is too high a price." He produced the manuscript from a drawer in his desk, sitting down with Lila standing beside him and Arthur sitting on the other side of the desk. She felt tall in her heels, and relished the feeling while Lincoln and Arthur remained seated.

"You do realize that spiritual books are making a resurgence?" challenged Arthur.

"True, but spirituality books often face dry periods of selling," interjected Lila. "Many authors wait months after the initial spike in popularity until they are well-known again."

Arthur was ready for a challenge. "Those dry periods don't typically last that long."

"You're mistaken, Mr. Samson. Those already well established in the religious and spiritual genres achieve repeated success and financial gain. Those just starting out have a long period of waiting for notoriety after the first successful publication. In a business to make money, one does make an investment, but throw out more cash than necessary when neither parties win out?"

Arthur paused for a moment. "A point well made, but what will Sterling get in return for lowering our company's desired price? Hypothetically."

Lila turned to Lincoln for any suggestions. "What about offering a one-on-one with the author of the manuscript?"

"Not a bad idea," Lincoln said as Arthur listened. "Bringing exposure to an up-and-coming writer would create lasting sales impressions, which in turn would bring continuous profit for Sterling, success for the emerging author—"

"Therefore encouraging the same author to keep submitting to the same publisher. In turn, everyone earns money and the genre continues with a steadier following. Profits on both sides." Lila's voice rose with anticipation.

"You make a stirring case," Arthur relayed. "I'm sure we can come up with a price everyone can be happy with. I wish I could still attest to the six hundred Little, Brown offered."

"What else is Little, Brown offering?" Lila added.

Arthur's eyes widened. "Excuse me?"

"For six hundred you're only getting the manuscript published. Does any of that six hundred come with advertisements or sample cover designs for the book?" A slight smile escaped Lila's lips. "Why not agree to a reduced price where other necessary expenses are covered with no additional costs needed to be taken out of pocket?"

"Are you both still going to offer the meager four hundred?" Arthur got up from his seat.

Lila turned to Lincoln.

"I think there's some room for negotiation," Lincoln remarked.

An agreement was made for the manuscript: $450, which included cover design samples, a short biography of the author, and social media advertisements. An hour and a half passed before Arthur Samson left Melville Publishing.

"You did good," Lincoln commented.

"Thanks." Lila blushed slightly.

"I've never seen Arthur so impressed."

"What do you mean?"

"He asked for your name before he left. It either means he wants to warn the head honcho about you for next time or to refer you to work for Sterling," interpreted Lincoln.

"Me, at Sterling?" Lila coughed.

"It's not the most far-fetched idea. You seem to fit in here and seem to thrive in a fast-paced environment."

"A chameleon changes its skin based on its environment."

"You're no chameleon."

Lila was desperate to change the topic of conversation. "Anymore meetings?"

"Another one in ten minutes, and then you have book-keeping until six."

"Has Walker said how long I will be here?"

"He called saying he wants you here no longer than a month."

"A month to be fully acquainted in administrative business?" *Is this the standard amount of time?* "Is that normal?"

"I believe so. Walker emailed me a screenshot of your résumé, and most of your experience already qualifies."

Back in her Brooklyn apartment, Lila stripped off her sweater dressed in a mosaic-like stain of ketchup and crushed hot dog from a teenager smelling of skunk weed. There was always something different occurring on the bus. The previous week, Lila had seen an old man stealing money from the purse of woman in a wheelchair. No one stopped him. As the stained sweater soaked in baking soda and water, Lila put a Lean Cuisine in the microwave and changed into an over-sized t-shirt and Hello Kitty shorts. She plopped herself on her weathered fabric sofa, finding sanctuary in her temporary home. It was no five-star hotel room, but it gave her the basics of a home; stability and her own bed to make as she saw fit.

"Welcome to Paris, girls!" Mrs. Goods announced when they all reached their four-star hotel. "We have big plans for everyone!

"Like what, Mommy?" Camille asked eagerly.

"Your father and I will be taking pictures of the architecture for a couple of days and you'll be joining us inside the Louvre," Mrs. Goods replied, taking out an expensive wide lens camera. It matched Mr. Goods's camera.

"What will we do while you're out?" Lila asked.

"You'll be with us still. You can explore and go into the shops while we work," offered Mr. Goods. "It won't take too long, and if you need to go back to the hotel, one of us can escort the both of you back so you two can relax."

"Can Lila and I rest for a bit?" Camille asked.

"Sure, and good timing too," Mrs. Goods replied, checking her watch and getting her camera ready. "The lighting is perfect, and I'm sure your father and I can get some great stills of the Eiffel Tower's info structure."

Camille went inside the hotel.

"Will you check in for us?" Mrs. Goods asked Lila, already handing her daughter her credit card.

"Sure."

"Thank you, Lila."

Inside the Hôtel du Louvre, Camille was attempting to speak to an immaculately dressed concierge behind a tan marble desk. Lila stepped in, having learned some French from the cassette tape in her Walkman. She told him her parents were at work.

"Notre mère n'est pas avec nous."

Lila and Camille looked up at the man.

Camille flipped through a French to English dictionary. "On...a faim." She placed a hand on her stomach.

"*Quel restaurant recommandez-vous?*" Lila handed the concierge her mom's credit card.

He seemed to pity the girls, aged twelve and eight, while accepting the credit card and giving them the room keys. He led the small girls to their rooms. The girls followed obediently.

The suite consisted of a mixture of pastels and browns, a large king-size bed, and a coffee table with lilac armchairs. There was a small desk adjacent to the bed and across from an adjoining door. On the other side was the room the girls would be staying in, but the only difference was there were two twin-sized beds. Everything inside the girls' side of the room was copied and pasted from their parents' room; the same Ebony-wood desk and coffee table, same colored armchairs, and same color-scheme of the room. The young bellboy, no older than eighteen, led the girls to their version of a minibar full of sweet candy and soda.

"*Merci,*" said Camille, sitting on her bed and trying to work the television. Using an English to French dictionary, she tried to decipher the channel listings. After a moment, she turned it onto a kid's channel playing "All in the Family" in French.

The bellboy came over and put on English subtitles for her leaving with a quick and polite nod.

Lila continued listening to her tape and Camille would be scanning her dictionary in between commercials.

By the early afternoon, Mr. and Mrs. Goods were still out on business, and the girls were getting hungry. Lila requested the concierge to recommend a place to eat. Before Camille or Lila could attempt to ask anything in French, the concierge left only to come back twenty minutes later with containers of food for them from Le Mesturet. For Camille, beef Tartare with potatoes and onions. For Lila, lasagna made with goat cheese and spinach. In a separate container, there were two slices of sponge cake and a variety of macaroons.

"Merci," responded Lila and Camille.

Lila went into the other room to get their mother's credit card and twenty Euros for a tip. The concierge, named Pierre, thanked the girls but refused to take their money. He had paid for their meal himself.

Even across the world, people feel sorry for us.

Checking her phone, there was an unopened text message from Lila's dad asking when if anything new was happening in her life and if she got her monthly check from them, an Evite from Camille for her latest fashion expo in Paris, a message from the Honda dealers that she was liable to trade in her car for a newer model (which she deleted), and a confirmation from Bank of America stating that her parents' monthly thousand dollar allowance was in her account.

They always insisted on snail mail checks, Lila recalled. Though their checks were a standard business-style, their penmanship was something Lila looked forward to the most. So ornate and beautiful; like that of calligraphy. Mr. Goods called it a "dying art." *The closest things to letters they send me.*

"People judge you on your handwriting," Dad told me once. I don't remember when. They used to write Cammy and me when they were on extended business trips, but the letters became less frequent. Unlike their checks. I guess it makes sense; they never really understood PayPal or thought it would lose their money.

At 7:30 PM, Lila tuned into "Jeopardy." It was the Teacher's Tournament. The winner was an English professor from NC State.

I wouldn't mind a free $33,971.

"Where's your sister?" Mom asked me during the Prize Puzzle segment on "Wheel of Fortune."

"*She's on a date with some guy in her Geometry class,*" I shrugged off.

"*Oh. Do you know when she will be back?*"

"*By nine, I think.*" Aren't you supposed to know this?

Mom turned to the TV. "What's the answer?"

"*Surfing on clear, blue waters,*" responded Lila. "*An island vacation most likely; Caribbean or Jamaica.*"

"*You should go on a game show, Lil. You're plenty smart enough. More than the rest of these guys.*"

She sat down with me. Kind of odd, but okay.

"*Maybe when I'm older.*"

"*I know you'll win.*"

"*What about Camille?*"

"*Um, between you and me, I think a game show would be too fast paced for your sister. She's smart, but you're sharp. If that makes sense.*"

I guess.

Lila answered yes and told her mom about her new opportunity. Her mother's response was a curt "Have fun."

"Typical," Lila sighed.

She returned her attention to the TV. Jay wouldn't be back until the next morning to move out more of her belongings. Lila enjoyed the silence, only to retreat into her room after an hour. She slept with meditation music for ambiance.

"What's the low down?" Walker asked.

"Lila's great, man," said Lincoln. "She just implemented a new method of categorizing books so we find them faster and provide more notice when we're running low."

Walker choked. "Really?"

"Yeah. I mean, I thought her thing about memorizing our system in a week was a front. I don't know why you kept her as a lowly grammar checker," relayed Lincoln. "I'm debating whether or not to send her to Harper or Sterling myself."

"Tell me you're joking," Walker nearly growled. "She works for *me*."

"I've already got an offer from Sterling Publishing a few minutes ago asking if she would be interested in being their travel writer. Paid vacation, benefits, and she has her choice assignments. Seems like anyone's dream job."

"What did she have to say to that?"

"I haven't told her yet, but hearing that new job offer will make her rethink her old job. What do you have to offer her? Chances are you're not going to follow through with giving her the position she deserves."

Walker's composure was slipping. "Get her back here by the end of the month. You're in no position to move her to another job. She's under *my* authority."

Lincoln couldn't let Lila go back there. There was a pause before he responded back. "Oh, no! Lila forgot to record the latest order history transactions! Goddammit, Lila! Nearly two weeks worth gone! GONE! She has to stay here longer."

It was futile.

"You were always a bad liar. Bring her back on the first of the month. Don't forget: I'm the one in charge of her. She's not your responsibility." Walker hung up.

He won. Lincoln had no choice. Leaving his office, he asked Lila to organize the latest books, shelve them, and call Harper to set up an appointment to discuss buying a new manuscript for the fantasy division of the company. Watching Lila work happily and without a second thought made Lincoln's heart ache. As Walker so bluntly said, Lincoln had no corporate authority over her. Everything was under Walker's demands, and Lila would be returning back to a meaningless job under the man with a Napoleon complex. All he could do was pray that Lila would get out of Foot in the Sand before her dreams and ambition were washed away.

The first of May was a bittersweet goodbye for Lila. She had gotten the necessary experience to secure a Head Editor position, but wished she didn't have to say goodbye to those who helped her; specifically Lincoln and Greta. For her goodbye, Stevie and his wife Joanne, who worked in Melville as the social media coordinator, baked Lila a two-layer marble cake as the IT technician Herbert and payroll manager Phoebe gave Lila a two hundred dollar bonus from their own commission bonuses.

"Keep it for a rainy day," whispered Phoebe.

By noon, a taxi had arrived to bring Lila back to Foot in the Sand Publishing. After sentimental goodbyes and empty promises to get together "one day", an impatient driver urged Lila inside the cab. Apparently he was under strict orders from Walker to bring her back before his own lunch break was over. Lila didn't know if it was out of concern or because she was desperately needed back. Her soon-to-be former co-workers thought of an entirely reason. Had they seen the chaotic scene back at Foot in the Sand, they would have been right.

Phones were ringing frantically, the employees were anxiously searching through towers of manuscripts, files were misplaced or missing with several interns anxiously trying to return them to their rightful places, and the twinge of hopelessness and unease was thick. Before she could find her desk under the mass hysteria of the office, Walker grabbed her out of nowhere and pulled her into his office, which looked as disorganized and disordered as the rest of the workplace, not to mention himself. His shirt was un-tucked, hair a mess from what Lila assumed to be from Walker grabbing at it, and his face appeared to be caked in dry sweat.

"What happened when I was gone?" Lila stammered.

"I got a new girl to train, but she never came on time, so she was let go. Searched for someone else, and thought he was going great. He *fortunately* got projects done on time, but HR told me to fire him as he lied about having a police record. Tax evasion," Walker explained. "You need to get to work *now*."

"What about the promotion you promised me?" was what Lila wanted to ask. Instead, she maneuvered her way back to her cubicle. On her desk was a stack of paper far exceeding the capacity of her wire copyholder to the point of the memos nearing the toppling point, her collection of pens and high-lighters absent from her designated cup, and a multitude of colored Post-Its expressing varying degrees of urgent notices and tasks needing completion. Lila's promotion would have to wait.

At 7:32 PM, Lila's iPhone notified her of a mass work email.

From: Walker Johnson
FWD Subject: How to Bring this Back Around
Date: May 2, 2017
To: FTS Workers

It's going to take a few weeks to get everything in order again. I'm expecting our team to not be opposed to working later hours in addition to working weekends. This will be paid, of course. Things got a little out of hand this past month, and I don't want to lose any one else. You're all great, and I apologize in advance for any inconveniences this news brings.

I'll notify everyone when everything is in order again and when everyone can go back to his or her orig-inal scheduled hours. A separate attachment will be sent to each individual detailing what responsibilities they will have. Some may be above and/or below their job description, but I implore that I need ALL OF THE HELP I can get from everyone.

In addition, there will be some new faces in the crowd; temporary employees and interns to help out with the more menial tasks and responsibilities. No need to worry, everyone else's jobs isn't in danger. No one is going to be replaced. We are all a family.

—*Best wishes*—

Johnson Walker, Founder/Executive Manager of Foot in the Sand Publishing, Co.

While eating microwaved macaroni and cheese for dinner again and watching a rerun of "Days of Our Lives", Lila felt as if everything she witnessed was her fault.

Things were never like that when I was copy editor; accepted manuscripts were delivered in a timely fashion and I already knew what the company didn't allow, Lila pouted internally. *If I move up, who will replace me? Clearly Walker hasn't had much luck in that department. A ditz and an ex-con, he said. He clearly needs me as a copy editor. I guess being Editor In-Chief will have to wait. If I get to be a commissioning editor, I'll settle for it.*

"You get out of there, yet?" Jay asked, yawning slightly over the phone.

"No, but I'm getting promoted soon," Lila replied. *I think.*

Lila could hear Jay rolling her eyes.

"This is different. I got the training I needed and firsthand experience negotiating as a commission editor. Walker has to promote me now. He promised."

"*Ay, niña.* You're ruining your life!"

"Please just be happy for me. I'm getting my life together to get what I want."

"You can do that away from Walks-All-Over-You."

Lila wanted to the topic to shift to Jay's wedding plans, but she knew Jay would want her to promise that she'd leave. "I'll play it by ear," she blurted out before hanging up, not wanting to hear Jay scream at her in Spanish.

They didn't even get to the wedding plans. Lila reminded herself to ask Jay the next time she came by to gather her belongings.

Sleep never came to Lila. She stared up at her barren ceiling blankly and scrolled through the latest pictures her dad sent of himself and her mom on an African safari until the first beam of morning light poked through her blinds. Putting on a blazer and blue shift dress, Lila ignored her drowsiness, put her sensible flats, and drove her Civic. By 1:00 PM, a small dent was made in finding the misplaced manuscripts and correcting the misfiled invoices. When it was Lila's turn to get lunch, she made her voyage to her usual hot dog cart. Johnny was there to greet her.

"Where've you been? I've missed you this past month." Johnny made Lila her usual. "You shrunk."

"Temporarily transferred to work at Melville. Got that administrative experience," Lila answered, handing Johnny a five. She didn't notice Johnny's last comment.

"Congrats! I take it you're the new one in charge?"

Lila's face fell. Johnny attempted to take back his assumption and give Lila her change, but she merely took her hot dog and left.

Finishing it by the time she made it back to her cubicle, Lila forced herself to shut out the noise of chaos and disorder around her to get her share of the work done for the day. Maybe then she could get back to her empty apartment early enough to prepare dinner as opposed to ordering delivery or microwaving something.

Alas it wasn't meant to be. Lila arrived home at 9:47 PM for a dinner of canned peaches and popcorn to watch the last ten minutes of "The Big Bang Theory." In between commercials, Lila took out the garbage and edited several manuscripts. Anything to speed up progress to achieve an eventual promotion. By midnight, Lila went to bed. She dreamt of nothing but darkness. There was a light at the other end no smaller than the head of a pin. By the time Lila woke up, it was the size of a grain of rice.

True to Walker's word, normalcy was achieved in several weeks time. The temporary employees were paid for their service and the interns received their necessary experience and/or education credits by the end of June. However, Walker was hesitant to grant Lila her much deserved promotion.

"But I did everything. I went to Melville like you told me to do. I kept records, held meetings and conferences, sold manuscripts.... What more do you want from me?"

"I would hire you, but—"

"But what?"

"I hired Stevens as Editor In-Chief while you were gone," admitted Walker, looking down at pre-approved manuscript. "He's been doing great."

A lump began forming in Lila's throat.

"I know I promised you the job, but I meant for it to be temporary at the time… until you came back. I swear.".

A look on his Swiss watch indicated he was through talking.

"You can have an early lunch break if you want. It's slow here; no more meetings and the newest manuscripts don't arrive until closing. Enjoy an hour lunch, Goods. Take a cab to that new Thai place on the edge of town; seems like your type of place."

Lila went into the women's bathroom. Picking the stall furthest from the door, Lila wept. Johnny didn't charge her for her usual; he could probably see the puffiness and slight redness around Lila's eyes.

"What was I thinking?" she sighed to him. "He's never going to think I'm good enough."

"He let you go out there," responded Johnny, shooing away a potential customer. "You can get an administrative job anywhere you want now."

"But Foot in the Sand is all I know." Lila wiped away another tear.

"Bullshit." Johnny slammed a fist on the counter. A ketchup bottle rolled off and onto the sidewalk. "You know that other place you went to and hobnobbed with the big boys, didn't you? Work there."

"I was temp. They won't take me back."

Lila knelt down, retrieving the ketchup bottle before leaving. Johnny groaned a thank you, muttering to himself as Lila made her way back to her stagnant office job.

"Fine, L. I hope you like living in stale tranquility."

"Bad day, again?" Tracy, Lila's almost middle-aged co-worker a cubicle down, asked once Lila returned from her lunch break.

She nodded.

Tracy handed her co-worker a napkin, which Lila took. "Look, we all have bad days, but if I were you, I'd try to get out of here."

The whites in Lila's eyes amplified. "Don't you love it here?"

"I did. I had dreams of writing for this place, but they say you're skills are better suited below what you know you can do.

They keep you complacent, offer you bonuses here and there, give you more responsibilities in the hope of moving on up, but all the while; you're in that same menial position one you started with, if not one above."

"Why are you telling me this?"

"I've seen you slave away in this job for almost five years; you've gone above and beyond. Two of the larger branches wanted you to work for *them*. Chief Editor and travel writer."

Eyes widened, Lila dropped her cup of coffee on the edge of her desk, ignoring it staining the carpet below. "WHAT?!!?"

"Oh." Tracy realized she opened a can of worms. "Walker didn't tell you…"

"What do you know?" Lila was restraining herself from the possibly of wrapping her long fingers around Walker's thick neck.

"Sit down first."

Grumbling, Lila sat in her cubicle as Tracy stepped in.

"Elaine got a call from the former head editor for Sterling asking about you. He apparently found some of your older, previously published work and wanted you to work for him at his company as their travel writer. Super Kush job, too," Tracy explained. "Everything paid for and your choice of pieces to write."

Lila rose from her chair, catching the attention of an apprehensive Walker. "Why wasn't I informed of this?"

"Elaine passed the message along, but I guess Walker overheard it somehow and intercepted it," assumed Tracy, rising as well to get Lila to sit back down. Her attempts were not successful.

Walker noticed this from the small window on his office door. He grew anxious and debated whether or not to hide in his office.

"Who offered the editor in chief position?" Lila's tone dripped in misery.

"Um, either Penguin or Harper."

Lila's typist hands formed fists, her nails digging into her palms to where the skin was about to give way.

"Take a breath," advised Tracy, which Lila did do. "If you want to talk to him, you have the advantage." She pointed to Walker recognizably trying to act as if someone was on the other line of his business phone. "Pull out your inner *American Beauty*-era Kevin Spacey."

Lila took it upon herself to barge into Walker's office, not bothering to knock on his door, which was unlocked.

"I take it Tracy informed you of my executive decision?" Walker stammered, clearing his throat as Lila glared at him from the entryway of his desk. He was still sitting at his desk.

Lila nodded. "When did they call?"

"About two months ago," responded Walker, attempting to mask his nervousness. "I was talking to one of the bosses of Sterling Publishing when your name came up. He asked Laney to deliver a message to you. I listened in, hit redial, and told him you didn't want to move to a new place and were happy here."

"So, let me get this straight: you did this deed *without* any consulting or approval from me?" Lila pressed, sitting down on one of the nearby sofas and crossing her legs authoritatively.

"I did." Walker's tone quivered slightly, but he remained upright.

"I see." Lila got up from the sofa and strolled slowly to Walker's desk pressing her palms on top of a manuscript she had finished proofreading. "And why, might I ask, did you such a thing without my knowledge, let alone my approval?"

"I hardly think you're in any position to question me." Walker rose up, towering over the petite Lila and her three-inch heels, yet she remained unrelenting.

35

"That's not an answer."

"You won't fit in a megacorporation when you can barely speak your mind here," Walker retaliated. He leaned closer to her and moved the manuscript out from her hands. His eyes and voice turned hard as steel. "You know I'm right, so don't try and blame me for making a decision where you would've said the same thing."

"Oh! And you were ready and willing to extend my sentence here. In a position you know is below me. Whether or not you knew that this would come back to me, which I know you know."

Walker pointed an accusatory finger at Lila. "Don't you *dare* use *my own* words against me. You seem to forget who signs your paycheck."

Lila took a deep breath, carefully preparing her final statement. "You seem to forget who has given you bestsellers and never made any mistakes."

"You—"

Lila held her hand up, interrupting Walker. "I have the gumption to be editor in-chief after the stunt I pulled earlier. It also appears I know what FTS represents as our conglomerate approved a manuscript that *didn't* go through *you*. Remember?"

"You are dangerously close to being fired." Walker's voice was voice low and unflinching.

"Then I quit," stated Lila. "You prevented me from a better jobs, and made executive decisions for others while blaming them." She turned her phone toward Walker, showing him a detailed Facebook post.

Everything she mentioned, in addition to more than Walker himself knew Lila was aware of, was written out; as detailed as any writer could make it.

Walker trembled.

"I also know about you and Scarlett's 'business trips' in Vegas to meet with the fictitious Mr. Scotts from Penguin. I wonder how *Jolene* will take it." Lila sat back down. "You shouldn't have made me in charge of bookkeeping."

"Why are you telling me this? You don't even like Jolene," Walker argued, his words shaky.

"I know. I just want you to know I know. It's damaging, isn't it?" finished Lila.

"It might bring this company into bankruptcy if that goes public. Not to mention, end my marriage."

Walker paused for a moment. "I'll cut you a deal."

Lila was taken aback. "I'm listening."

"I'll promote Tracy and give her a contact that will buy her screenplay." Walker used her fingers to number off his proposals. "Second, I'll write the most glowing recommendation for Sterling Publishing. I'm sure they'll work something out."

Lila nodded in compliance.

"Third, I buy Jolene a dozen roses everyday."

Poor Scarlett, that unfortunate whore.

Lila was curious as to how much further Walker was willing to go, but pushing the limits might make things worse for her. He had the power to keep her running.

"Thank you."

Walker sighed heavily. He had clearly been defeated. "Are you sure this is what you want?"

Just have Lilia nodded. "You know I'm better than this."

A slight, tense pause came between the two. Neither knew if the other was going to speak up. Once Walker grumbled under his breath, Lila bit the bullet and spoke up before Walker had the luxury.

"You promoted Stevens over me. He nearly caused FTS to recall all of our copies of *A Guide to Your Own Mount Sina*."

"Honest mistake," Walker attempted to brush off.

"The copies came out as *A Guide to Your Own Mount China*."

Lila remained eerily calm; something startling Walker.

"We are able to fix it and market the manuscript as a self-help book about finding the secret to love and happiness through Chinese philosophies."

It was at that moment where Lila's temperament shifted. Her eyes grew wide and vicious. They were trained on Walker; he couldn't escape her.

"*You* did *nothing. You* weren't there when the shipment had to be recalled so it could be rewritten, edited, approved, and re-shipped. *You* didn't even catch the mistake. Tracy did. She, Steve, and I stayed up for *weeks* on end to have it shipped without this company getting into trouble with our conglomerates." Lila's voice began rising quickly. "*We* did all that *without* being paid overtime! *We* made it our bestseller! For eighteen months! All you did was take credit!"

"Are you done?" Walker asked, clearing his throat and sitting up at his desk.

"With you, I am. Give me what I asked for and what I deserve," ordered Lila.

"Alright, Goods." Walker pulled out the company checkbook. "You're really set on burning bridges here."

"I'm just someone who doesn't have anything to lose anymore," concluded Lila.

II

East of Eden

"Is something wrong?" Mr. Goods asked. "It's not Wednesday."

"I know. It's my job," Lila replied.

"What happened?" Mrs. Goods asked, clearly in a rush.

"I quit."

Her parents were preparing their cameras for their latest assignment.

"You did *what*?" Mrs. Goods shrieked. "What were you thinking? Do you know how hard it was for you to get that job?"

"I got it after graduation and after two other interviews, Mom. I don't think that constitutes a struggle in the job market," retorted Lila.

"Don't talk like that," Mr. Good interjected. "Finding another job, especially after the stunt you pulled with your boss, won't be an easy feat."

"I'm aware. I've already posted an ad for another roommate to help with the rent and I have an interview lined up for this week. I made sure my old boss called them to let them know what he did," explained Lila, suppressing a groan. *They were never like this with Camille.*

"Tell us what happened, Cammy," Lila's mother said, sitting with her daughter and husband in the living room as Lila read East of Eden.

"I quit my job at Winterfell Fashions. I told them I was better than someone who brings them their coffee," Camille declared. "I told them I was going to run my own fashion line."

"That's great, honey, but how are you going to get the money and experience for that?" Frank asked.

"That's where my trust comes in," continued Camille eagerly. "I want to use some of my money to go to fashion school in Italy. Only the best go there. I'm torn between Istituto Maragoni and Ferrari Fashion School."

A slight pause between Mr. and Mrs. Goods. Lila looked up from her book to see what was going to happen next.

"We're going to support this choice, but you need to learn Italian before you go," concluded Karen. "We'll hire you a tutor, and you can spend your gap year learning the language."

"What?" cried Lila. "You can't be serious."

"We are. What's the problem with that?" Mr. Goods returned, confused with his older daughter's outburst.

"I don't remember the both of you being this relaxed when I told you I wanted to go to college in New York."

"You're young, Lil. You can't just automatically say one thing when chances are you're going to change your mind," excused Mr. Goods.

"When have I been known to change my mind?"

"Lila Elaine, don't you sass me. Why can't you be happy for your sister?" Mrs. Goods pressed. "She's going for what she wants."

"Like she did before; the jewelry business, the online hair barrette shop, the sushi place the previous owners were putting up for sale, a greeting card company—"

Camille sprung up from her seat. "Shut up, Lila! Just stop it! I know what I want to do now. So put your bitterness where I won't see it again!"

Mr. and Mrs. Goods ordered the girls into their own rooms until dinnertime. The parents found a tutor for Camille and Lila was forbidden from going to a foreign film festival the upcoming weekend.

There would be an upcoming conversation concerning the seriousness of Lila's choice to go to college in New York. Another week would pass before Mr. and Mrs. Goods would acquiesce to Lila's desire under the condition she call them at least once every week, or text them if they happen to be travelling for National Geographic.

"New York is a dangerous place," Mrs. Good warned. "I don't want you going out to places you don't know or hanging around degenerate types."

"Yes, Mom," said Lila.

"Don't go out at night, always keep your phone and money on you, and don't forget your pepper spray," continued Mr. Goods.

"Yes, Dad."

"Make sure you get a job, either on campus or near it, so you have money to spend on yourself. You're still going to have your trust and monthly allowance, but we want you to understand the value of hard work," pressed Mrs. Goods.

"I will." I already have a summer internship with the town Mayor and a part-time job as a barista.

"Are you listening to us, young lady?" Mrs. Goods shrieked again. "What plans do you have for this? Are you truly prepared for this waiting game? You know we're in a recession, don't you?"

"I'm going to be okay; I have enough in my savings. Don't worry about me. Tell Camille I won't be able to make it to her fashion exposé—"

Throwing out Camille's name did the trick. The conversation shifted focus to the successful and talented Camille. Mr. and Mrs. Goods went on for about ten minutes about "disappointed and crushed" Camille would be at "her own sister" for not being there on her "big day." Lila listened for a little while longer before finding an appropriate amount of time to end the call and pick out the most business-like outfit from her closest to wear for the interview. By the next morning, she would've changed her outfit another five times only to go back to the original outfit she chose: a sleeveless red dress reaching just above her knees, a brown cardigan with a metallic belt over her waist, and a pair of brown knee-high boots.

Looking out of her car window in between stop sings and traffic lights of Manhattan, Lila watched towering buildings encompassed of mostly windows and steel zipped past her. Passing a score of coffee shops, Lila drove past a set of high-end department stores where the buildings were painted silver and gold. Even the nearby chain restaurants looked like copies of the Louvre. A green light signaled Lila to continue her drive.

"Your résumé is quite impressive, Ms. Goods," replied Mrs. Poole, the chestnut-haired hiring manager of undeterminable age. "Why did you stay at Foot in the Sand for long?"

Why did I stay in an office once serving as a printing press in the fifties? There were new warehouses added to update the building and make it appear successful, but every employee there knew FTS was just a small fish in a big pond. Everyone except me, until I peeked behind the curtain.

"Part of me thought I would have the chance to move on up, but I stopped and settled," Lila answered as honestly as she could.

"I heard," Mrs. Poole responded. "I have some good news and some bad news about the position previously offered to you."

"Tell me the good first." A bead of sweat ran down Lila's neck.

"We have a position for you here—"

"But it's not for the travel writer one?" assumed Lila.

Mrs. Poole shook her head.

"Head editor?" Lila squeaked.

Again, Mrs. Poole shook her head. "I'm sorry."

Lila's hopes were falling apart. "What position do you have available for me?"

"I want to put you in a more senior position."

Lila looked confused. "What do you mean?"

"You met our negotiator Arthur Samson, didn't you?"

Lila nodded.

"He would normally want someone to work for him as an editorial assistant—"

"That's entry level."

"I'm well aware," Mrs. Poole responded calmly, "but considering your extensive background knowledge in administration and types of trends correlating to the most book sales, Arthur has submitted your name in getting the job of his commissioning editor."

Lila gasped.

"I guess it's not professional for me to reveal such information, but it's just between us girls." Mrs. Poole turned to Lila's résumé. "Now, by the end of the day today, you will receive a phone call from me about the role of a commissioning editor along with what you'll be doing for the first few weeks if you decide to accept the job. Is the number on this current?"

"Yes."

"Do you have any more questions?"

"A couple. First, what about advancement?"

"Working as a commission editor is a stepping stone to becoming editor in-chief for the entire company. Additionally, being a commission editor would entail a bit of travel as you will be searching for authors to buy as well as articles and ideas for our literary magazine publisher in Boston."

"How much interaction will I have with authors and publishers?"

"Quite a lot, Ms. Goods. You will be meeting with our writers to assist them in meeting deadlines while meeting with our corporate bookkeeper upstate to review developing trends for what our audience will most likely to respond to."

"Thank you, Mrs. Poole."

"My pleasure. If you have any more questions, Arthur will be heading to lunch in a few minutes. Perhaps you could hang around here and join him to get a better idea of the tasks he'll be giving you."

Lila's eyes widened and a bead of cold sweat ran down her forehead to her neck. *Please don't let it be like that episode of "Polly's World" where her boss makes her go on a date with him to get promoted. It didn't end well for her when she said no. Had to move back in with her brother and fiancé for the next three episodes until her boss died and she was able to take his job. Still don't know how that happened.*

"Thanks for taking me," Camille said, her voice sugary sweet for a twenty-year-old. "I don't want my tutor to wait."

"Dare I ask why you need me to drive you when you have a car and a license?" Lila stopped at a red light.

"My license is somewhere in my room. I think it's in my laundry basket or in one of my other pairs of pants."

Eye roll moment. "How long are you seeing your tutor?" The alleged tutor was her new boyfriend for the month.

"A couple hours. I'll call you when I need you."

"What am I supposed to do until then?"

"Go out with his brother. He's a year older than you."

"I'm not being pimped out."

"Come on, Lil. You need to get to dating or you're going to end up alone."

"It sounds a bit out of my comfort zone."

"Oh. My apologies, Ms. Goods. It's nothing like that, I assure you. Arthur always maintains a strict professional relationship with his co-workers and colleagues," assured Mrs. Poole. "He'd quit his job before breaking that trust. His office is down the hall, second door on the right. Door should be open."

A welcome notion, considering how bad things might have gotten.

The women shook hands and Lila left the office. True to Mrs. Poole's word, the office door was open and Arthur Samson was inside. He was putting on an expensively crafted sport's jacket in preparation to leave when he noticed Lila.

"So Sterling hired you?" he said.

"Not that I'm aware of. Um, Mrs. Poole told me to see you about what working for you would entail," countered Lila. "She also told me to join you for a business lunch."

Arthur raised a slightly skeptical eyebrow. "That's all she's intending for us?"

"God, I hope so."

Arthur's eyebrow remained raised. "What's that supposed to mean?"

Lila's cheeks turned crimson as she rushed to find the right words to erase her immediate scoff. "I didn't mean for it to sound like that. You seem like a nice guy. Intimidating, but Mrs. Poole said you maintain a professional relationship with everyone around you, and I don't want to come across as some little thing trying to sleep her way up the corporate ladder—"

Arthur cracked a smirk and raised his hand to stop Lila's babbling. "I'm joking. Calm down, Goods."

"Lila."

"What?"

"If I end up working for you, I'd rather be called Lila."

"Fair enough." Arthur was heading out of his office. Lila stepped aside to give him room. "Do you like Italian food?" he asked her, motioning Lila to join him.

"Yes."

"Come on, we'll take the company car."

Holy shit!

Everything about Sterling Publishing looked more modern, extravagant, and luxurious compared to Foot in the Sand. The inside of the building consisted of large windows and pristine white walls. The desks in the larger workspace were brand new ebony-wood desks with personal compartments holding files, magazines, and personal décor. On the tops of the desks were Apple computers, matching printers and scanners, silver office phones, and personal knickknacks and photos. Each person, though not the textbook-definition of happy, looked determined and passionate about whatever his or her jobs entailed. The attire was sharp, immaculate, and powerful. Lila didn't want to get on the wrong side of any one of them. The youngest of the employees, possibly a year or two younger than Lila, strutted along the workspace and handled seemingly important files so casually that Lila couldn't help but envy him. Even the parking lot in the back of the building felt as if it had been repainted and renovated fairly recently.

The company car, parked in a space labeled "Arthur R. Samson", was a sleek black 2015 Series 7 Beamer with the Sterling Publishing logo on both sides. Arthur's gesture of opening the passenger door for Lila nearly made her feel like he cared about her, but his silence told her that any conversations the two might have would strictly be about business. To Lila, he didn't seem like the type of person she'd want to discuss any random occurrences in her life.

"Ever been to Patsy's?" asked Arthur, startling Lila as she looked out the window at the passing buildings decorated in a variety of glass, brick, and steel.

Lila shook her head. "It's not the type of place I can go to on a regular basis."

"Order what you want. You need it."

"Excuse me?"

"You look like you eat like bird. Get some meat on your bones." Arthur's tone was still professional, yet he was acting like a father to Lila.

"My old roommate used to do most of the cooking. Since she left, I've mostly been microwaving Lean Cuisines." *Why did I tell him that? He's going to think I'm poor!*

A pained look came across Arthur's face. "You need some real food, Lila." There was a light strain in his voice as Lila's name left his stern, thin lips. "Don't look at the prices."

How did he know? "Why? You're buying?"

"Yes, and no it's not a date. I'm trying to be courteous. I'm a business man first, but also a man who treats a young woman with respect."

"Sorry."

Arthur was taken aback. "For what?"

"For any offense I might have caused."

"None taken."

From the outside, Patsy's Italian Restaurant commanded a presence. The large black canopy up front paired with its bold, white lettering made it so anyone walking or driving by would notice it. The green neon lettering illuminated slightly in the early afternoon sun and a large front window displayed newspaper clippings of town events, an A grade from the Health Inspector, and photos of the employees. The inside caught Lila off guard. The shaded chandeliers created a warm and intimate atmosphere. On each of the cherry wood tables were fresh cream linens with napkins folded into what looked like crowns, modestly plain china plates and wine glasses, and small porcelain vases holding lilies.

Arthur wasn't inside for half a minute before a middle-aged maître de escorted the two to a table where two glasses of red and white wine were presented along with a pair of menus. Lila sat down and observed the menu. Some of the prices were just as outrageous as before; the appetizers were close to or were twenty dollars, and the least expensive entrée was twenty-three dollars. Lila could've ordered any of the vegetable dishes and get change back, but one doesn't go to an Italian restaurant for the intent to eat mindfully.

"Welcome to Patsy's. I'm Allison, and I'll be your server. Can I start you off with anything?" greeted a redheaded waitress in her thirties who clearly enjoyed the food at the restaurant.

"What's your soup of the day?" inquired Lila.

"A halibut chowder," Allison replied.

"I'll have that."

"Make it two," said Arthur.

After a lunch of Veal Francese and Filet Mignon Marsala, Arthur picked up the bill as promised without so much as glancing twice at the total amount he was handing over. The jovial and portly head chef, Sal, greeted Arthur affectionately. Sal then acknowledged Lila's presence.

"She's cute," Sal replied with a grin. "She tied you down?"

"She's my new commissioning editor," Arthur said. His voice was cool.

"Good luck," Sal joked.

Arthur dropped Lila off at Sterling where she got in her car, said a quick goodbye, and left.

As Lila began making herself stovetop macaroni and cheese, she got a call from Camille. A rarity.

"Mommy told me you weren't going to make my fashion show."

Hello to you, sis. "I'm in the middle of looking for a new job, and I think I found it," explained Lila.

"It's always work for you. You never have any fun." Camille's voice was soft and baby-like. "Take a vacation, Lil. Or a work retreat if *that* will get you out here. I want my baby sister with me to show her support."

Lila could feel herself giving in. "Why do you want me there? You know I don't really care about high fashion."

"You work yourself near death and you never take any time for yourself. Get some R and R in another country." Camille was becoming more insistent.

"I don't really know much Italian."

"It's okay, I'll be your interpreter. It's similar to Spanish; the language you took all four years of high school and college." The last part of the sentence was spoken with an edge of bitterness Lila deciphered immediately, but she chose not to call Camille out on it.

Lila sighed. "When is the fashion thing?"

"Two months from tomorrow. Get a ticket as soon as you can, while they're affordable."

"I'm not poor, you know? I just choose to use my trust fund responsibly."

"I do, too. You know that, right?"

You started using it before I ever knew about mine. "I remember you using it a lot, that's all."

"I used it for school!" Camille sounded sweetly devastated. "Just come and spend time with me. Please?"

The other line went dead. Lila threw her cell phone at her sofa and tended to her juvenile dinner. On TV was a new "Wheel of Fortune" with Vanna White wearing a gold gown with a sparkling corset design. The prize puzzle was a trip to Aruba and the big prize for the final round was a red 2017 Hyundai Avante. Per usual, Lila solved each puzzle in four letters or less. She could've solved the last puzzle if it hadn't been for the phone call from her dad.

She blabbed. "Hi, Dad."

"What did you say to Camille?" Mr. Goods demanded. "She called us *in tears.*"

Always the drama queen. "I didn't do anything. All I said was I couldn't go to Italy, because I've got a job to find and I don't fit into her high-end fashion world," Lila attempted to explain.

Mr. Good continued after a short pause. "She told us you seemed ungrateful for the invite."

"Of course not," assured Lila. "Camille said I would have to buy my own ticket. I actually was planning on going, and she wants me to come."

"Why would she say something like that?"

"She might have insinuated that I'm poor by choice."

"You're not poor, Lila; you have a trust."

"I know that, Dad. Camille does, too. I choose to only use it for emergencies."

"Sounds like a smart thing to do, but don't think you can't use it. You've known about your trust since your sixteenth birthday. You're not the kind of person to spend it all on something stupid, and I trust you."

"Thanks, Dad." *One of the nicest things he's ever told me.* "I still don't think Camille would want me at her event anyway."

"Let me have a talk with her; she'll come around. Your mom's leaning a bit toward her side, but I doubt you'd start a fight with Camille."

Of course not. "Thanks, Dad. I'll let you know if I got the job."

"Thanks, Lily-Bug. Have a nice night. Love you."

"Love you, too."

Lila was free to watch "Jeopardy's" Teacher's Tournament. The teachers on the show were from rural, underprivileged areas and them being on the show was for the purpose of providing their schools with basic necessities for their students. Even during Final Jeopardy, those who wouldn't be returning for the next round would be leaving with a minimum of two thousand dollars. It was one of the few times Lila was caught off guard with a game show.

Considering that the next day was Saturday, Lila stayed up later to watch classic sitcoms she and Camille used to watch. As the first episode of "Full House" went into commercial, Lila received the coveted phone call from Sterling announcing what Lila had already been told: she was to work for Arthur as his commissioning editor starting the upcoming Monday. During the weekend, Lila spent most of her time organizing her closet and putting anything she thought was unprofessional and juvenile in a donation box. She was an adult now.

Updating her status on her Facebook brought the news of Jay taking photos of her bikini clad fiancée at her family's summer home in California along with possible ideas for their upcoming wedding. The two messaged idea back and forth about ideas for centerpieces before Jay decided to forgo them entirely.

"It's clichéd," she reasoned.

Two hours passed before Lila received a notification from a potential roommate to confirm a 3:30 PM meeting and interview for the next day.

"Here's your desk, keep all personal knickknacks and mementos tasteful, you get a forty-five minute lunch, and every Friday there's a pool for use of vulgar language on the secretary's desk," Arthur explained, pointing at a large mason jar with various coins and bills inside. "Olivia keeps track on the frequency everyone uses unprofessional language, and the loser gets everyone coffee at the end of the work week."

"I don't curse," stated Lila, sitting down at her mahogany desk standing outside of Arthur's door.

"Then you don't have to worry about buying coffee for the staff. Hope you enjoy it here," responded Arthur, heading into his office and leaving the door half-open.

Lila had begun logging current trends in book sales on her office iMac when she received a phone call from Foot in the Sand Publishing. Walker was on the other end with a welcoming and humble sentiment: "You're welcome."

"Morning, Mr. Johnson. May I ask the reason for your call?"

A dramatic groan was heard before Walker replied back. "Calling to confirm that a manuscript from a 'Kyle Render' was sent to you."

Lila typed in something on her computer. "The manuscript was sent to us, and was given to Mr. Samson twenty minutes ago."

"Thank you. Enjoy your life, Burnham." Walker hung up.

Lila placed the phone back on the receiver to find Arthur standing over her. "You overheard the call, didn't you?"

Arthur nodded.

"Did I handle that wrong?"

"You handled it better than I would have. The president of the company has been contemplating dropping them for a little while, and this might be more incentive for him to go through with it."

"Walker kind of reminds me of Nellie Olsen."

"Who's that?"

"A bully from 'Little House on the Prairie.' Girl with a rich-kid complex who always has to be better than everyone and keep others down."

"I thought you preferred 80s and 90s shows with a laugh track."

"Yes, but I read the books as a kid."

Arthur smirked. "Keep up the good work, Lila."

Three invoices and five appointments later, Lila checked out for work, took a cab home, and welcomed the silence of living alone. It wouldn't be until the next day when Lila received her monthly check from her parents, which she split between her checking and savings accounts. Car keys in her hand, Lila was about to leave to buy groceries when the potential roommate greeted her: a dark-haired, fair-skinned girl in her early twenties wearing an oversized NYU sweatshirt and skinny jeans.

"I almost couldn't find the place," the girl replied, stepping inside after Lila let her in. "It's a nice place though."

"Thanks."

The small talk was forced and awkward before the student, Anna, felt comfortable enough to ask Lila questions about inviting guests over, how much her share of the rent would be, and common roommate etiquette. Once Anna realized her share of the rent would be $1,515 as it had said on the notice posted on Lila's Facebook, she was hesitant to sign the lease.

"It's a little bit more than what my parents have been paying for me to stay on campus, give or take a thousand for the year. The drive isn't bad, but I still don't know," she went over.

"I understand."

It would be variations of the same story throughout the day: a woman in her thirties wanting a new place to stay but was strapped for cash as she was in the midst of a divorce and a 27-year-old earning her doctorate in neurobiology. The newest one was different: a man younger than Lila recently kicked out by his parents' for coming out.

"I'm not sending you to the streets. We can work something out," Lila offered.

"What do you mean?" The man was trying not to sound too hopeful, but couldn't help it.

"You can pay for groceries and clean up around the place; take out the garbage and such."

"I'll still look for a job. I promise."

"That'll be one of our hard rules, then. Do you have some sort of an account?"

"I withdrew everything I had before my parents could freeze my accounts. Five thousand and change." He pulled out a shoebox. "You're entitled to fifteen-hundred for my half of the rent."

"It'll be due at the end of the month."

"Lila, a word," Arthur stated, motioning her to his office. "What's this I see about taking a two-week vacation in September?" he asked once Lila was in his office sitting down.

"I'm visiting my family in Italy. My sister has an event there."

"I see. What kind of an event?" Arthur probed.

"A design showcase."

"Her designs, I assume?"

Lila nodded. "It'll be my first time seeing them."

Arthur raised a concerned eyebrow. "Your family or your sister's designs?"

"A bit of both."

There was a slight pause before Lila spoke up again.

"Am I approved to go?"

Arthur smiled slightly, nodding. "I understand the importance of family, but I'm not letting you go out there without some sort of an assignment."

"What do you have in mind? I'm up for anything."

"Since you are attending a showcase, you can do a journalistic piece detailing the world of high couture."

"Isn't the blonde guy from the business division doing that?"

"Parker, and yes. Management also wants another piece in a female perspective considering how they feel women are more in tuned with fashion trends."

Great. "I may not be the right girl for it, to be honest, Sir." Lila continued before Arthur had another chance to speak up. "I don't identify as being fashion-conscious like my sister. I maintain a comfortable and professional look, but that's as far as it goes."

Arthur was genuinely shocked. "Really? You're... um, you know—"

"A woman." Lila felt defeated.

"No. This isn't the fifties. With your sister being so involved in fashion, wouldn't some of it rub off on you?"

"No."

"Bookworm?"

Lila nodded.

"Well, considering this new development, you are...to... Milan?" Lila nodded. "Milan then. Send me a fax of your receipt, so it will be recorded as part of your travel expenses. You'll be reimbursed upon your arrival back to the states. You get to decide the piece you write on so long as it means something to you. Nothing half-assed."

"Yes, Sir."

"When you finish your piece, email it to me immediately. The absolute latest I'll accept is a week after your return. Five to seven pages or two thousand words. Judging from your past work, I have high expectations for you."

"Yes, Sir."

"I can't believe my baby sister is coming to see me!" squealed Camille, her voice going an octave higher than normal. "This is an especially important night for me. It could absolutely change my life, Lil. I've collaborated with a lot of designers, Vera Wang and Louboutin for instance, but this is my first solo project."

"Sounds good."

"I want everyone I love there. Mommy and Daddy will be finishing their stay in India and then stay in Tibet for a few days before they show up in Italy. I can't wait to have you, Mommy, and Daddy to myself. No work, no commitments, no deadlines. Let me know when you get on the plane."

Lila joined Ben on the couch, watching "Saved by the Bell" re-runs. "How's the job hunt going?"

"Not so good. Once the manager finds out I'm on the verge of being a dropout or gay, my hopes are dashed."

The social justice warrior from within stirred in Lila's stomach. "Don't you want to fight them about that? That's discrimination."

"If they don't want me working in fast food, then I'm not going to fight it. Maybe I'll have better luck in retail or Starbucks," moaned Ben.

"You should still fight it. They have no right—"

"It's not worth it to slave away for minimum wage and come back with grease burns on my arms."

"What will you do for money?"

"I still have my car. If things get worse, I can sell it and use whatever I get for it to hold me over."

"Let's hope it doesn't come to that. Um, you do the dishes and I'll get dinner."

"With whom are we meeting with today?" Arthur asked, greeting Lila by leaning over her desk.

"A Richard Irons about him missing his deadline for his new book at noon. This will be the second time he's done this. There is also a senior broad member from Boston dropping by around four to pick up the latest copies of Emerson Review," read Lila.

"Excellent. Have you given any thought regarding your assignment?"

"I'm not sure. I want to write about fashion, but I also want to write about my sister, but I've spent so much time editing. I wouldn't know how to separate them."

"Interesting concept. Elaborate for me."

"Well, the fashion industry is presented as cut-throat and unrestricted. There's so much pressure in succeeding when it seems like the entire world is watching your every move. My sister seems to handle everything in stride. Part of me wants to know how she does it, but I don't know how to handle being as creative as her."

"I can understand that. The concept sounds promising, but the piece may become one-dimensional and muddled. I would advise you to have moments where you and Camille have different views on fashion. Maybe a side-by-side comparison."

"That won't be a problem, Sir."

Lila's first paycheck arrived when she came home from work: Thirty-eight thousand dollars. On the back of the paycheck, Lila found a note Arthur had written out. His penmanship was sharp and fixed.

Mrs. Poole got a hold of your information before she hired you. Walker paid you shit. Included is a little extra you can use for your work trip and for what that brown stain should've paid you. Sterling will no longer be representing or accepting work from them and have since been transferred to Black Tar Literary Co.

Using her iPhone, Lila used her Bank of America app to deposit her latest check; snapping a picture and waited for the confirmation email. The next day, she'd transfer half of it to her savings just in case anything were to happen. She was told to be prepared.

The look on Ben's face was a mixture of exhaustion and minimal optimism. He had come back from a job interview to work register at a record store, but was rejected at Macy's.

"I'd earn hourly, plus commission. I don't have it in me to judge people into buying clothes they may not need."

Ben later got the job at Spin This! Records working register and stocks, but still faced the possibility of having to trade in his car for one with more gas mileage to afford his part of the rent and groceries along with dropping out of St. Lawrence. He had three thousand dollars left in his shoebox.

"Since you're leaving for Italy soon, what do you expect me to do?"

"Basically keep things in order, don't burn down the place, and no guests unless you run it by me," explained Lila. "I'll get you a spare key tomorrow after work. If you need anything more for your stay, you can get for yourself; clothes, food, and whatnot."

III

Do You Remember?

The Delta plane ride to Milan was a long one, but Lila was grateful for the upgrade to business class, as she didn't have to deal with crying infants and parents toning out the child's discomfort. Arriving at ten minutes to eight, Lila made her way to the bathroom to freshen up, change into a cleaner pair of clothes, and put away her audiocassette on learning Italian. After grabbing her luggage and finding the personal driver Camille sent for her, Lila was escorted to a silver Mercedes. The drive was silent; allowing Lila to observe the sun-kissed villa the driver was heading to. Everything around her looked simple and rustic, yet there was a natural beauty to it she never noticed in New York. New York was a city in constant construction with its surroundings made modernized for hopefuls or deterrents to remind one of what lay in the shadows of failure. Milan didn't seem to have shadows. Everything was open, despite the narrow streets. Lila felt happy and free, but would probably feel more so if she were there on her own. There were residents with still smiles and an essence of purity Lila couldn't explain.

Even the sun looked more pure, but it felt as if everything above her was indecisive. Most of the sky was a cerulean blue, but it seemed as if anywhere Lila was, the sky was ashy and neutral. She took pictures with her phone, sending them to her parents.

After about twenty minutes of window sightseeing, Lila arrived at a luxurious condominium in the midst of other identical cream-colored concrete buildings.

"Camille will be back in a few minutes," the driver said. "She went to the market to get some extra sheets. May I help you with your bags?"

"Please," replied Lila, taking one of the suitcases as the driver, Niles, took the other.

The inside of the condo was spacious and modern, but the décor was as vintage and rustic looking as the rest of the town. The walls were a pattern of dark off-white color with some white panels. The furniture, a couch and companion chair, shared the same off-white color, but the fabric contained specks of evergreen along with matching accents for the furniture to stand out. On a white shelf, Lila was treated to pictures of Camille shaking hands and smiling with Vera Wang, Christian Dior, Guccio Gucci, Christian Louboutin, and Giorgio Armani.

"Your room is down the hall and to the left," Niles informed. "You can leave your suitcases in there."

"Thank you."

Lila handed Niles five Euros before he left. Her room consisted of pale pink walls, a gold brass bed covered in royal purple silk bedding, and glass end tables. On the ceiling was a chrome LED-ceiling fan with foldable blades and chandelier-like crystal fixtures. The room starkly contrasted with the vintage-style condo, much like Lila and her sister. She wondered if Camille actually knew her or not; she despised anything pink, fluffy, and made to look like it was just for girls. Lila's room back home was more of a blend of bohemian and French styles. Her bedspread was a royal blue and silver paisley-patterned set purchased from Bed, Bath, & Beyond though she abstained from obtaining the decorative pillows. There was a simple desk in her room, though most of her work was done in the living room. The only decorations on her walls were her college diploma, a Monet and Van Gogh print, and a swap meet painting. Her temporary room had a gendered, princess-like quality making her uneasy. The bed wore a violet skirt with a light grey canopy hanging above the ceiling; the walls were lavender and white, and shimmering satin magenta decorative pillows. Lila was afraid to touch them; they most likely cost more than her half of the rent. She was already counting the moments to leave the room.

As Lila unpacked, the click and opening of the front door announced Camille's arrival. "Good morning, baby sister!" Her voice was as noxiously sweet as ever. "Did you get some breakfast?"

No. "I had a snack in the airport." Lila left her clothes on her bed.

"I would've made something. Oh! You look so cute!" She turned to Lila, hugging and catching her off guard. "I love your hair cut. Is it new?"

You haven't changed a bit. Lila brushed her brown hair to one side. "It's been like this for years."

"I'll miss your bangs," cooed Camille. "Make yourself at home, Lila. Do you need anything while you're here?"

"Some Excedrin would be nice. When is your fashion showcase?"

"It's tonight at six. There's also going to be a dinner and wine gathering. All the best designers and socialites will be there, and I want to show off my baby sister. Do you have a gown to wear?"

Yes, thought Lila. *My unicorn will bring it to me shortly.* "I don't know where to get one."

"I'll have one of my consultants send you one from our sample rack," decided Camille. "What color would you prefer?"

"Blue."

"Oh! I'll be wearing blue, too."

Scratch that. "Green or copper."

Camille smiled brightly. "Excellent choice. I can't wait to tell Mommy and Daddy you're here."

"Speaking of, where are they?"

"They're waiting for their transportation in Tibet. The pilot got sick and the two got another assignment from National Geographic, but I can live stream it for them," answered Camille, trying to sound cheerful. "They'll be so proud of me. I wish they could see us together though, bonding and sharing secrets. Do you think it'd be okay if I took a picture of us at the exposé to show them how happy we are?"

"Sure, Cammy."

"Ooooh! This is so exciting! We'll go get mani-pedis, go out to this little bistro I found, and tell each other what's new in our lives. It'll be perfect; like old times. Don't you think so, baby sister?"

Doubtful. "Possibly."

Camille playfully smacked Lila's arm. "You trickster."

The hours Lila spent shopping with Camille weren't as mind-numbing as she had predicted; Camille paid for mostly everything she felt Lila would need for her stay, the bistro's menu had a great variety of options, and the shops the two were in were as elite and classy as the shops portrayed in "Pretty Woman." Similar to the film, nearly every store clerk and manager rushed to Camille's aid ready for whatever her next order would be. Lila enjoyed the spillover perks, though part of her wished some of the sales women didn't speak Italian quickly in a vain attempt to confuse her.

"*Mi rendo conto che io sono magro,*" Lila spoke up, causing the sales women to turn crimson.

"What did you tell Martina and Francesca?" Camille whispered.

"That I know I'm skinny." She turned to Martina and Francesca as they brought over another pair of shoes. "*Grazie.*"

Once Lila and Camille finished their shopping spree, the two returned to the condo to get dressed for the showcase. Camille's mood grew more elated at the thought of her newest designs being her ticket for more recognition to the board of directors and for Lila to see what she had been working on for several months.

"Oh, Lila, this day will be life-changing. Everything is on the line, but I'm ready," she repeated to Lila and to herself. "Have Mommy and Daddy called?"

Lila shook her head. Camille's exhilaration faded quickly.

"Maybe they're already there. Didn't you did tell them where it was being held?"

Camille became blissful again. "I did. You're right. Mommy and Daddy wouldn't miss this for anything."

Lila saw the naïve optimism in Camille's eyes as a limo drove the girls to a gray marble building where a cluster of photographers snapped pictures of Camille and asked her about Lila. Camille was dressed in a pale blue satin gown with crystal straps hanging at her alabaster shoulders. Her hair was in an elegant French twist with jeweled barrettes. Meanwhile, Lila was adorned in an evergreen silk gown with a fitted bodice and apron-like neckline supported by spaghetti straps crossing atop the gown's sultry open back. The billowing maxi-style skirt cascading from the elasticized waistline made Lila feel more out of place and princess-like. The gold headband tiara didn't help matters either. She never had anyone give her attention like this; she felt like she mattered. Like they were seeing her beauty, though she would never try to compete with Camille.

"Hello?" a fourteen-year-old Lila greeted over the landline.

"Yeah, um I was calling for Camille," Tom, Joe, or Fred stated, almost insulted that Lila was on the other side.

"She's out on a date right now. Can I leave a message?"

"I wanted to take her to the movies next Sunday."

Lila wrote down the message. "Can I get a name? She has many other offers."

"Fred, but since she's busy, you want to go out with me?"

Lila hung up, and tore up the message.

"Who is this?" a middle-aged gentleman in an Armani suit asked Camille, facing Lila.

"This is my baby sister Lila. Isn't she pretty?"

"Certainly a lovely woman," said the man. "If she were taller, she'd be a model." He turned to face Lila, only to return his attention back to Camille. "Such a shame."

Just because I am plain, short, and not at your tastes, doesn't mean I'm deaf, Lila internalized, taking a glass of rose-hued champagne for herself. "I don't like being disrespected."

"Yes, but please don't make a scene," pleaded Camille. "Complain about it later, please?"

Lila groaned.

The Armani Man came back in Camille and Lila's direction, but he came with a purpose. He barely glanced at Lila when he gave a note to Camille and left to talk with a tall blonde with a tanning bed hue to her skin and hair extensions.

"Mommy and Daddy are stuck in Tibet. There's a protest, and their plane won't be able to make a landing until next week," stuttered Camille, still smiling for everyone else. "Will you live stream the show for them?"

Lila nodded. She half-expected their mom and dad to not show up considering the last-minute note being the only other word from them both girls received. They weren't always the best at communicating.

The Armani man and three other Armani clones walked her and Camille's way. Based on the look on Camille's face, the others had to be from the Board of Directors.

"*Ciao, Bella,*" the oldest looking Armani man greeted Camille. He turned to Lila. "*Ciao, miss.*"

"*Ciao,*" both sisters responded.

"This is your special day," the eldest man stated, putting his heavy arm around an anxious Camille. "Ready a take the biggest chance of your career?"

Camille nodded slightly, shifting slightly away from the older man, but enough for him to notice.

"How is this?" the younger man asked, looking at Lila in a way that she couldn't decipher if he was leering at her or just acknowledging her.

"Lila." She put her hand out to shake, which the man did in slight surprise. "*Io sono sorella di Camille.*"

"You best find your reserved seat," the younger man stated. "The show is going to start in a few minutes. Giorgio will escort you."

The last Armani clone motioned Lila to follow him to a cluster of seats marked "reserved." He was polite and shy around her; he didn't make a move Lila could interpret as rude and worth a right hook. The two engaged in small talk before the others arrived for the show. Camille took a seat a chair away from the eldest gentleman, but he still remained close enough to her where Lila could see him enforce some sort of authority over Camille. She remained calm, but still looked uncomfortable and on the edge of her seat.

A minute passed before a remix of the most popular songs announced the start of Camille's first solo showcase. Camille squeaked in delight until she received a stern look from one of the suits. Lila had never seen her sister look so eager before. She became excited for her. When the first skinny, gorgeous model arrived on the runway in an organza gown the color of starlight ordained in ivory floral appliques, the crowd went silent. The clicking of cameras and murmurs ranging from confusion to condemnation echoed throughout the auditorium. Lila took notes on a small notepad she snuck into her clutch purse. She circled observations she thought sounded the best.

"I swear I saw that same color in the Adolfo line up back in '85," one of the suits whispered.

"I thought it was Ralph Lauren circa 2007," another said.

Camille was embarrassed and wanted the show to end. It did after two hours.

"What happened out there?" one of the Armani clones demanded Camille as Lila watched from the bar. "Were *any* of those your own designs?"

Camille nodded in fearful silence.

"Everything you shared were carbon copies of nearly every designer you've worked with! That drop-waist A-line gown was clearly a blend of Dolce & Gabbana and Versace!" another man exclaimed. "They'll be disappointed to know you've stolen from them. I hope Calvin Klein doesn't see your copying their signature scooped neckline on your last piece."

"I would never do such a thing." Camille's voice was shaky.

The youngest Armani said, "It looks as if we were wrong to take a chance on you. *Vergognoso.*"

Lila continued listening in.

A man in his early thirties with dark hair sat next to her. "*Ciao.*"

"*Ciao.*" Lila put her notepad down.

"I've never seen you here before," he replied. "Jerome."

"Lila."

"Beautiful name. Sounds smart."

Lila blushed.

"You should come around more often. Maybe I could be the one who buys you a drink."

"I think this may be a one time thing for me."

"Such a shame."

When Jerome left, Camille was still being scolded. During this time, Lila pulled the small notepad from her clutch out again and resumed writing down her observations, specifically the bits and pieces of conversations she could decipher from Camille's superiors and members Lila assumed were high enough on the A-list to be invited or were the arm candy of someone on the A-list.

Camille a fraud??

Need to prove oneself in a cutthroat world

Designs were beautiful and took time to complete, but not enough for Camille

Is she imperfect??

When the sisters returned to the condo, Camille made a beeline to her room. Two faint clicks indicated her locking her bedroom door and turning off the light. Lila took it as a sign to start a draft of her article. The first thing written was the title: "In the World of Fashion, It's All About Who You Know." It wouldn't be until three in the morning when Lila decided to get some sleep. She left the living room, taking her laptop with her, and collapsed into her silk sheets. It wouldn't be until the following afternoon when Lila woke up to Camille and three other women in the condo.

"What's going on?" she asked Camille.

"My assistants Isabella and Alessia." Camille pointed to two young-looking twin brunettes wearing baby pink cardigans and pencil skirts. "And my associate Katarina are here to help me brainstorm new designs." Katarina was the only one Lila could tell apart; she was blonde and looked like she enjoyed daily meals.

"You're getting another showcase?"

Part of Lila wanted to hope for the best for Camille.

"I'm optimistic they'll give me another chance. These pieces will be better, and my own," Camille replied.

"*Chi è lei?*" Katarina asked Camille.

Lila answered for her. "*Io sono sorella di Camille.*" She turned to Camille. "I'll leave you all alone. I'm going to go into town."

"Have fun, baby sister."

Lila entered her new world in a pair of faded capris, ankle boots, a violet blouse, and a pullover sweater. The air was turning cold and off-white clouds covered nearly every inch of the sky above her, but Lila ignored it. Her hair was swept to one side as she made her way from the condo to a rustic and intimate café where she enjoyed a cappuccino and biscotti.

"It's pure, not like that swill you Americans drink," an elderly Italian man replied.

"*Supponi che io sono un americano?*" Lila retorted, sipping her cappuccino and paying the man.

"*Sì.* You're new. What brings you here?"

"My sister. She had a big showcase the other night, and she's working on new designs right now."

"You two aren't spending time together?"

Lila was warmed by the fact that the elderly man didn't name Camille.

"I don't know. She seemed excited to have me around, but now she's going to be absorbed in her work."

"So you know the pattern? Why else come here?"

"My boss wants me to do a piece about my sister and the fashion industry."

"I see. Who's really absorbed in their work now?"

"It's not like that."

The man raised a skeptical eyebrow.

"I wanted my sister to show me around," Lila continued. "I told her I was going out, but she didn't offer to come or tell me to stay safe. Granted, I would've, but it still would have been nice to hear Camille say it."

After several hours of sampling in recommended restaurants and purchasing high-end labels, Lila headed back to the apartment when she received a call from her mom.

"How was the showcase?" she asked.

"The designs weren't received well," Lila answered, not surprised by the lack of a hello.

"Poor Cammy. Tell her that her mom and dad send her our best." Mrs. Goods was inappropriately cheery.

"I will."

"I hope the two of you are having fun."

"Doing some shopping right now, then we'll head back to her place."

"I'm jealous. Your father and I send our best."

"Thanks, Mom."

The faint *click* from the other end indicated Mrs. Goods had received enough information to pass along to Mr. Goods to assuage their guilt. Lila was welcome by Camille and the same the entourage of fashionable and glamorous women. In light of company staying, Lila stayed in her clothes for the rest of the evening as opposed to giving into her desire to change into an oversized t-shirt and pants with an elastic waist. Granted, she was nowhere near as stylish as the fashion elite, but Lila could pretend for a little while longer. Her sister would comment about Lila exchanging her public clothes for "unkempt" private ones once the others left. When they did leave, Camille left the new designs on the coffee table and had Lila pick up dinner from a local pizzeria.

Lila was all too happy to leave. So much so that she forgot her phone.

"What in the world is this?" shrieked Camille after Lila came back with a pizza. She was pointing to an email Lila got from Arthur on the phone.

Judging by how close Camille was to saying hell, Lila knew it was serious.

"It's from my boss, and why were you going through my phone?"

Lila sett the pizza down and snatching her phone away.

"Your boss called twice. At least, I figured out he was your boss. So to be polite I answered for you, explained to him who I was, and he proceeded to tell me about an article you're writing about me." Camille's sweet voice turned sour, causing Lila to sweat anxiously.

"What?"

"I asked what article, and he proceeds to tell me that you're writing a piece about my job, my life, and...here's the icing on the cake…*my disastrous showcase.*" A smile of betrayal spread across Camille's now imperfect face. "I know everything, Lil. You didn't close the file you wrote notes on for the article and you didn't password protect your phone. Rookie mistake."

Lila wanted to be mad at Camille for invading her privacy, but it still would have stung Camille once the article was syndicated. The distance could have been her saving grace.

"I've been nothing but nice to you; trying to bond with you and going the extra mile to make sure you were comfortable, but it was all for nothing." Camille sighed. "I wanted us to be sisters."

"Why?"

The question took Lila and Camille by surprise.

"That's what we are. Aren't we?"

"We share certain chromosomes, but other than that I can't say."

Camille was on the verge of tears. "Do you want us to have a relationship at all?"

"I don't know, probably. Why do you want one so bad? It's not like we've ever been close. *That* can't come as a shock to you. I come here, and you act all phony and sweet like our relationship was as corny and sweet like a nineties sitcom. You give me some attention, then you go right back to work and act like I don't exist."

Camille was enraged. "Don't you pin this on me! *You're* the one at fault here."

"Maybe if you tried to make me feel like you gave a genuine damn about me! You soak up any attention given to you, and leave me on the sidelines. It's been like that since we were kids. Apparently all of Mom and Dad's attention couldn't satisfy you."

Camille's slender fingers curled into her palms and her eyes showed evidence of holding back tears. With one more expletive declaration, Camille stormed into her room and slammed the door behind her. Lila took the pizza with her into her own room, eating the entire pie out of spite before sleeping.

The girls didn't speak to each other for a week and kept texts between their parents brief and mundane. If any plans were made, they were made as a way to avoid the company of another. Lila spent her time at the same local coffee shop talking about life and politics with the elderly man and his wife, Angelina. When she wasn't in town browsing stores or purchasing items with Camille's special discounts, Lila barricaded herself in her room and opened up her Hulu account to watch "Saved by the Bell" and "Polly's World." She could care less that Camille was spending more time at her job than at home. The sounds of the door opening and closing were her indications of Camille leaving and coming back. Both girls made it a point to cook meals after the other had eaten, or to play it safe, eat out.

During the moments Camille did have her assistants in the condo, Lila wore her baggy pajamas with pride, strutting into the kitchen taking ten minutes to get leftovers or make a sandwich much to Camille's chagrin. It wasn't as if Camille could do anything out of spite other than give Lila the silent treatment, which seemed to suit Lila just fine. It didn't feel as much of a punishment Camille hoped it would be. Lila enjoyed the silence, and her anger seemed to fuel her desire to finish her article. It became more scathing and resentful towards the fashion mogul. The following Wednesday, Lila sent the first draft to Arthur before she left the condo to Ristorante Da Puccini. Unfortunately, Camille was there with the Armani men. Not wanting to leave just yet, Lila requested a seat far away from her sister.

After a silent meal of Parmesan swordfish with arugula, seafood risotto, and beat beef with spinach, Lila got a piece of tiramisu to go before hailing a taxi to go back to the condo. The driver was silent and the ride was smooth, allowing Lila to gaze out of the window at the sprinkles of light coming from the streetlights. Exiting the cab, Lila was blanketed in blackness and silence. She appreciated it when the taxi driver stayed along the curb with the headlights on until she was back inside the condo. No one was home, and Lila took full advantage of re-mote privileges. She turned on Camille's TV first to a collection of older episodes of "Wheel of Fortune." Three vacation trips to tropical hard to pronounce islands, five car giveaways, and a lost chance at fifty thousand dollars. A predictable formula.

When she grew tired of correctly guessing the puzzles, Lila found a throwback classic's channel showing marathons of "Full House", "Growing Pains", and "Polly's World." Lila would've been thrilled, but each episode had mature, intense moments. Stephanie had a classmate who was being abused at home and was forced to keep it secret, Dj had to drive a drunk Kimmy Gibbler home as Dj's mom died because of a drunk driver, Mike ran out of a party where cocaine was present, and Polly had to decide whether or not to defend her former col-league who murdered her assailant in self defense.

"Your client knowingly acquired a firearm illegally, thus breaking the guidelines of her parole," the sleazy, by-the-book lawyer argued to Polly.

"So does that give that predator the right to harm her? Are you saying you want that scum to still be alive?" shrieked Polly, her face turning pink in frustration. *"A woman protecting herself is less important than that man's life?"*

"Your client broke the law," the lawyer reminded, rising from his desk. *"A fact me and my correspondent won't be shy at revealing*

and one you can't hide. If you bring this case to trial, don't think this won't damage your reputation."

"Even in television, women are trapped," Lila muttered to herself.

It was past midnight when Camille tried sneaking into the condo only to wake up Lila.

"You stayed up?"

Lila nodded. *She's talking to me.*

"For me?" Camille looked surprised, but flattered.

"You said you'd be back by eleven. What happened?"

"Giorgio and Paolo called me to discuss my career. And whether or not I should have one."

"Oh my—" Lila sat up on the sofa.

"I still have my job, but it wasn't easy for me to convince them."

"What do you mean? You convinced Mom and Dad to give me your car and get a motorcycle license when you moved here."

"The kind of agreements I made back home are different from the ones I make here." Camille sat beside Lila, dress inching up her thighs. "They told me they took a chance with my designs, and the lack of positive reviews from them made them doubt my talents and dedication to the field."

"But—"

Camille held up her hand to silence Lila. "What I'm about to tell you cannot leave this room."

Oh, no. "Why?"

Camille forced herself to keep her answer short. "I had to convince them that I'm worth… keeping."

"What did they make you do?"

"Nothing I can say right now. I want to put it in the back of my mind for now."

"You need to—"

Camille shushed her. "No one can know! This stays here!"

"But it could happen again! Camille you have to—"

"I *have* to keep my mouth shut and keep my job. I shouldn't have told you. Now you're going to judge me."

"I'm not! Those men are rats, and you're defending them gives them power to—"

Camille began weeping. "Just shut up! Just shut up! You don't know everything! Go to bed and leave me alone!"

Neither of the girls slept well that night. Both cried themselves to sleep; Camille over her actions to keep her job, and Lila for not knowing the atrocities Camille suffered through alone and further degrading Camille for the sake of publication.

It was as if all of Milan felt lost and confused. The sun was a muted yellow amongst the steel gray clouds hovering over the small Milan villa. The sky wasn't an ocean blue, as it had been during Lila's stay.

Waking up in her princess-style room to the sound of clamoring pots and pans was more refreshing to Lila than the sounds of heated honking cars, loud small talk, and the occasional siren. She got out of her purple silk sheets to the sight of Camille cracking eggs over a skillet and a plate of blueberry pancakes on the counter. The card beside the short stack indicated the pancakes were for Lila.

"You're not mad at me?" Lila asked, inspecting the warm and fluffy freckled pancakes.

Camille shook her head; her back was still toward Lila.

Lila sat down at the counter, pulling the plate close to her. "Are we going to tell Mom and Dad what happened?"

Camille shook her head again.

"What *do* we tell Mom and Dad?"

"Nothing," stated Camille, transferring her eggs onto a plain white plate. "I don't think they ought to know."

"Why not?"

Lila began digging into her pancakes. They tasted heavenly.

"Mommy and Daddy have a particular image of each of us, and I think we best maintain that image to the best of our abilities. I think it would be best that neither of us tamper with how Mommy and Daddy choose to remember us." Camille's tone feigned positivity.

Lila nearly choked on her bite of breakfast. "So, just let them remember you as the flighty one who eventually found her calling, and me as the smart one?"

Camille nodded, forcing a smile. "It's better this way."

"For us or for them?"

Camille dropped her optimism and cheeriness. Her expression shifted to a bleak and hopeless epiphany. "Does it matter?"

Lila didn't have the heart to argue further. "Are you going to be happy about this?"

"No, but my job will keep my mind occupied. Since my negative reviews on my showcase, I can make myself busy by improving my designs and looking more at what's selling and what will be making a comeback." Camille tried to smile again, but ceased the effort. "It will work for an undeterminable amount of time. When those bad memories creep up on me, I'll shift my focus on the good parts. It's something that's served me well in the past, Lila. Have you ever tried it?"

"I have few good memories of us to use."

"Edit them."

"Is that what you're going to do with what happened earlier?"

Camille nodded and shook her head. "I'll remember it between us, but when the family is together, I'll tell them we bonded and we're closer than ever. The fight won't exist in their world."

"But it's normal for sisters to fight."

"Don't say that, Lil. We were supposed to get along, but something happened. I don't know what, but I think it started when I was in high school."

Lila pushed aside her breakfast. "What do you mean?"

"I was pretty. Gorgeous even. Everyone always said that, but nobody ever told me if I was anything else. I could paint and draw, which got me attention from Mommy and Daddy. I enjoyed it. I was good at it. Even they said so." Camille smiled a sad smile.

"I remember."

"Yet, I don't think it was good enough. I wanted to show them I could do more than scribble. When they took us to France, I wanted to buy a cassette to learn some basic French. They told me not to bother. When we got there, I could pick up phrases and new words, but no one really cared to hear me speak. Everything was just given to me; no questions asked."

"I remember."

"Suddenly, I was bombarded with college brochures my last two years of high school. *Then* I was told I had to decide on a career. I had to figure out what I was good at doing and what future it could and would bring me. Not everything was going to be given to me anymore."

Lila listened, glued to her seat.

"I joined the most elite-looking clubs, made the right friends, networked with the teachers who liked me, but I didn't please Mommy and Daddy the way you did."

"What do you mean?" Lila squeaked. "All they ever did was talk about you."

Camille looked genuinely surprised.

"It was always you who had her pictures on the wall, and it was always you they showed off to whenever they were home. They would say hi to me, but they always had time for you."

"Because I was a part of so many activities, Lil. I also wanted them to not be mad at me whenever I quit one. I was so afraid of letting them down; them being disappointed in me. I wanted them to think I had figured my life out the way you did."

"What?"

"You already knew what you wanted to do. You knew what college you wanted to attend, what you were going to study, their criteria for merit scholarships and grants, how you were going to earn your way. *You* were what Mommy and Daddy expected of *me.* They told me that I had to get my life together the way you did."

Lila had to hide her inner joy. "Really?"

Camille nodded. "First I wanted to be one of the youngest people in the world to own and run a business. That would've surely made Mommy and Daddy proud. When the first one failed, I thought that I just chose the wrong business. Neither one worked for me. Mom and Dad were supportive, but deep down, they wanted me to settle down and come to a final decision. They got tired of watching me fail over and over. I saw it."

"That's when you chose fashion?"

Camille nodded. "I thought it suited me; I love shopping, I know what looks good with what, and I made a couple things I wore back then. When they knew I made a final decision, they were so happy for me. It felt like I was as valuable a daughter to them as you."

Lila's eyes grew wide.

"You were the smart one, the sensible one, and the most mature. I was always so jealous of your writing abilities and the awards you got. Heck, your first published article from college was reprinted in *The New Yorker. The Atlantic* even wanted it.

You were already on the path to greatness while I was struggling to keep my head above water." Camille started smiling, only for it to turn wicked, grim, and demented. "I fought to keep up with my wise and gifted *younger* sister! How…how pathetic is that?! *I* was supposed to be the golden child!"

Camille pounded a tight and ghostly fist into the counter, sending her breakfast flying before it splattered over the floor. Lila rushed to her side and led her to the living room sofa as Camille grabbed one of the decorative pillows, attempting to rip it into however many pieces she saw fit. Lila snatched it away, but Camille still had her feverish desire to break something. Lila handed her a framed picture of their family when Camille was nine and Lila was five, but the picture didn't collide into the wall. Camille pressed the photo between her arms and heaving heart. Her eyes were glazed with tears.

"They wanted…to come," she wept. "They were supposed to be here."

"Things happened out of their control," Lila offered, placing a soft hand on her sister's shoulder.

"They took on that other assignment," revealed Camille. "They could've left, but they didn't."

Lila suddenly wanted to break the photo, but comforting her sorrowful sister was more important. "But they—"

"I'm not good enough for them, Lila. Even now. Money is no problem for them. We have trusts and they have a nice home. For them to miss one assignment wouldn't be a big loss for them. They *chose* to stay longer. Maybe there was a plane mishap, but I'm not putting my money on it."

"Why wouldn't they see it? They've always gone before, haven't they?"

Camille wiped away a tear. "Barely the amount of fingers on one hand."

"But you said…"

Camille looked up to face Lila. Streams of tears flowed down her cheeks. "All I wanted was my family there, but it was too much for you all. The one time I got *you* here, you were going to slander my name. You can't imagine how I must feel. I just want them to be proud of me."

"I do." Lila put the photo back on one of the end tables and sat closer to Camille. Years of bottled jealousy and ire had been released. Lila felt closer to her, but also felt halfway across the world from her. "What do we do now?"

"Are you still going to send that slam article to your boss?"

Lila shook her head. "I'll write another one. I don't want that article to be the last thing you remember from me."

"Thanks, baby sister. Do you think you could ever make time for me?"

Lila reasoned she could spare her sister a phone call or text message about her day at work and asking for advice on dating if she decided to try it out again. It seemed like a sisterly thing to do. It might become a ritual to speak to each other and become more sisterly. "Yes, Camille."

"I'll do the same."

"What about Mom and Dad?"

Lila immediately wished she could take the words back, but was surprised when Camille seemed unfazed. She was already altering their emotional moment.

"They'll be happy to know that we're going to make more time for one other. It'll give them some peace of mind. I don't ever want them to think we can't get along."

They're never going to know about this, Lila promised, facing her now calm and smiling sister.

"Want to get some lunch?"

"It's ten in the morning."

"Then we can do a little window shopping beforehand. When's your flight back?"

"Sunday."

Sunday came and both sisters were at Milan Malpensa Airport. They said their goodbyes, and Lila began making her way to the gate. She texted Ben to see if he could pick her up, but he said he'd be pulling an extra shift down at the record store. Rather than call a shuttle so late into the trip back, she called Jay who was happy to hear from her and give her a ride back.

While waiting for the plane, Lila read an email from Arthur concerning her draft she received the previous night.

> *From: Arthur Samson*
> *Subject: Notes on your draft*
> *Date: September 12, 2017*
> *To: Lila Goods*
>
> *I received your initial draft of your story. It caught me off guard when I first read it; I could feel the passion and intensity in your writing. It makes you stand out, and corporate seems to like your fiery spirit. However, there is the concern about the article coming across as one-sided and possibly slanderous. I hope you have given clearance to write the article so long as the accounts are true.*
>
> *The first draft of your article has been sent to our conglomerates. The overall consensus is that your article has been approved for publication. A couple of administration staff has requested you edit your article. An achievement to celebrate, no doubt.*

I was caught off-guard. I never thought about you sending an article so salacious and saucy. You are full of surprises. Since you have sent the article earlier than anticipated, you have an additional three days to review your material.

Respond to this email to verify you are aware of what you've read and if you wish to retract the article. No questions will be asked.

Arthur R. Samson
Chief Editor/Head of Sterling Publishing, Co.

Lila wondered what Arthur meant in his email. Normally congratulatory emails were easy and formulaic. His was making her think.

They like me. Or the angry me, anyway. Well, it can't be too bad, can it? Is that why I became a writer?

"I liked your poem, baby sister," said Camille over the phone, reading her sister's piece in a local magazine. *"Not bad for seventeen."*

"Thanks, sis."

"It sounds like you. Not depressing, but honest."

"Did you like the line about the way one looks at the sun?"

"Loved it. I hope someone looks at me like that. Totally and completely exposed."

Before the plane took off, Lila managed to type out a quick reply on her phone. As she was about to press send, an overtly perky flight attendant bombarded her and ordered Lila to put her phone away. Lila hit the send button, and complied with the flight attendant's pushy request.

From: Lila Goods
Subject: RE: Notes on your draft
Date: September 13, 2017
To: Arthur Samson

I'm honored that my article has been approved for publishing. Thank you so much for giving me this opportunity. I would like to add a few more things to make the article less one-sided. Since I've submitted the previous article, new information and circumstances have given me cause to alter some details. Please give me this chance. Don't withdraw the article. I want it to be something I can be proud of.

Lila E. Goods
Commissioning Editor to Arthur R. Samson: Chief Editor/Head of Sterling Publishing, Co.

Plugging her charger into an outlet, Lila was able to finish her marathon of "Saved by the Bell" while catching up on "Jeopardy" Ben had recorded for her. The flight attendant was nowhere in sight. When she had finished the recorded episodes, Lila opened the article she had originally sent and proceeded to delete all but one of the seven pages.

Part of me will always look at my older sister in envy and bewilderment; she fits in any place she goes, attracts attention most women crave, and has more drive and ambition in her field than I've ever seen her have growing up. ...
What changed was the time we spent apart. ...
Diving into her world, I was immediately greeted by immaculately dressed men and women catering to me almost as much

they catered to my sister. There was still something off. I was called skinny and small more than I was called beautiful. Camille was the one noted for her beauty and potential status as arm candy.

… She had her first solo showcase after collaborating with names I've only seen on tags of clothes I get secondhand. They commended her bravery....

Once again, the same flight attendant ordered her to put her phone away. Lila ignored the attendant and began watching puppy videos on YouTube. He had enough, and left her alone. He was still obligated to refill Lila's drinks, give her the in-flight meal, and ask if she needed an extra pillow. All the while, she was on her phone catching up emails and text messages. The last text message she sent was to Camille.

Know that I'm sorry and it's okay to remember.

"How was visiting Miss Perfect?" Jay asked during a round of drinks at the Recharging Station Tavern.

Lila was going over vows Jay had written on a piece of yellow pad paper. "Unexpected," she answered honestly while reading the last few lines.

"I find that hard to believe. Let me guess," Jay responded, pondering her list. "She was all sweet and phony, and she got mad at you for calling her out on it."

"Yes and no. I did, don't get me wrong, but I didn't feel any better about it. I wanted her to feel as hurt as I was, but she was feeling that hurt and so more without me knowing it."

"What could ruin her?" Jay scoffed. "Milan's made you soft, *amiga*. I thought you hated Camille."

"I don't think I ever did, but I could never hate her now. If I did, I think I would turn into one of those people joining a cause for the sake of being part of it to avoid the hypocrisy of supporting it in all actuality." Lila handed back Jay's vows. "They're great."

Jay sipped her Lemon Drop, smirking. "Thanks. And this is why Sterling hired you. What went on to where you're sympathetic toward Camille?"

"I empathized with her."

Jay nearly choked on her drink. "How? She's a fashion designer. You're a writer...editor technically, but you know what I mean."

"I know, but seeing her fail and finding out what she had to go through to keep her job made me want to be a mother to her," explained Lila, handing Jay a napkin. "She had a showcase, and her designs weren't as big of a hit as she thought they would be."

"So what?"

"Part of me was happy that things weren't going her way, but when she told me the lengths she had to go to in order to keep her job and to prove that she is passionate about it, it resonated with me."

"*Explicar.*"

"Never mind. I shouldn't be telling you anyway. I promised her."

Jay looked confused, but didn't want to press the matter further. "So what's your plan now? Do you know what you're going to write about?"

"No."

"Then get on it, because I need to tell you what's going in my life for a change."

Jay drove Lila back to the apartment they once shared. Ben, eating microwaved macaroni and cheese in sweatpants, greeted them. The television was turned to CNN's take on the latest incident of mass violence. As per the routine, two of the news anchors were offering empty thoughts and prayers.

"How was work?" Lila asked, moving her suitcase to her room.

"Okay. I'm thinking about getting another job," Ben sighed.

"Why?" asked Lila, changing her clothes on the other side of the closed door.

"The record store pays a little above minimum wage, but I need more so I don't depend on the last of my box," explained Ben.

"Mix drinks," Jay offered before waving goodbye to the new roommate. "*Adios, chica.*"

"Sorry about that," Lila responded.

"No, it's okay. I can go into the Barnes and Noble and buy *The Joy of Mixology.*"

"Or download the PDF."

"Studying to get a job making minimum wage and tips. Welcome to my life."

Before Lila returned to work, she retreated to her quiet area: the most remote corner of Sal's Subs and Hoagies with the most optimal Wi-Fi. With her usual meatball hero with extra marinara sauce, Lila felt the most prepared to tackle her article. Her new goal was making Camille come across as relatable and a possibly sympathetic. Fingers pressed onto the keyboard at a leisurely pace, but Lila typed each word with purpose. She didn't want her article to be rushed and hackneyed.

"How much progress has been made on the piece?" Arthur asked, standing over Lila at her desk. "You are aware that you are under a strict deadline? No extensions and no exceptions unless you somehow injure yourself to the point where you can't type."

"I'm aware, Mr. Samson," responded Lila, her eyes on her computer screen. "I've been working on it in between organizing our appointments with our contributors and managing our submission page with the IT guy."

Pleasantly amazed, Arthur soon returned to his office as Lila typed away and put one of her ear buds back in and tuned her playlist to a collection of 80s one-hit wonders. Anytime Arthur left to attend to new hopefuls that day, Lila followed close by and was mindful to keep her iPod hidden under her desk and under her purse. Arthur seemed to notice, but as long as Lila was being productive, he wouldn't confront her.

Entering ~~the world of~~ Milan was leaving the big pond of New York and entering into an even bigger pond. (~~Even so,~~) the new pond felt comforting. The part of yourself that tells you to not go certain places after dark had temporarily subsided ~~with~~(in me). I only read about paradise, but I seldom experience it. The idea of paradise only continued when I arrived at my sister's. Fame treats her well, but she was modest about it.
    ~~All my life~~
    ~~For as long as I can~~ ??
    Seeing the simple and beautiful city contrasted with the sister I thought I was familiar with and who grew up alongside me. (Maybe) Seeing my sister was as if time stood still. Camille was still beautiful, feminine, and graceful. Making it worse was how she seemed to not know it; despite the attention she regularly received from men and ~~a couple~~ women.

While relaxing in the apartment, Lila got a text from Ben saying he'd be working late. With this, Lila made a phone call to Camille momentarily forgetting the time difference. The late hour in Italy was confirmed with Camille's yawning on the other line.

"Is something wrong?"

"Not really. I wanted to ask you a few questions," Lila reasoned.

"About what?"

"How you got started, and how you were able to work with those I saw in your pictures."

"Oh! Well, I met Vera Wang first. I was a consultant at the time, and Vera saw some of my earliest designs."

"Did you become a consultant for her?"

"Yes and no. She became a mentor for me, and her latest showcase for wedding dresses became a co-collaboration. Since my name was next to hers, others wanted to get to know me."

Lila began writing down Camille's responses in a notebook. "How did you meet Vera?"

"Giorgio arranged it for me," Camille answered a bit too quickly.

"How did that happen, Cammy?"

"Nothing, I promise. He saw potential in me."

"Camille. It's okay to tell me. I won't judge you."

There was a short pause over the phone. "It's not me I don't want to you to judge, but...I got to work with Vera because I had to fire someone."

Lila wrote inscribed the response quickly. "That doesn't sound too bad. Isn't it part of your job description?"

"Yes, but I had to fire someone who was competent. I liked having him around. He was nice and had ambition, but he wasn't a big-breasted girl who could barely get a coffee order right yet whose uncle is a big contributor to our fundraisers got the job. She still has it, even though she's caused some close calls with misinterpreting sales figures."

"But...never mind." Lila continued writing down Camille's responses, noting the changes of inflection in her voice. "How did you come to meet the others? Dior, Armani, and Gucci among the others? Did something familiar have to happen for you to get the chance to with them or to talk with them?"

"One of them I went on a date with Paolo, but it ended up not being so bad. We still are close, but sometimes work and romance don't really mix. Paolo and I do the best we can to make it work."

"How do you guys manage it?"

"Through work and dedication."

"Camille. I want you to be honest. It's okay to tell me."

Another short pause.

"It's been hard for us to be serious about our relationship. Mutually. Considering how much I have to do to be taken seriously."

Lila ceased her writing momentarily. "Like what?"

"Me having to dedicate a lot of time to my work, which is expected, but maybe it's more than I should be. The others have time to relax and spend with their friends and family."

"You're just ambitious. There isn't anything wrong with that," reasoned Lila, as she resumed writing down her sister's responses.

"But I didn't want to fire that guy, and I don't want to have to go on pity dates to be taken seriously. I hate being compelled to compromise my integrity, in *any* way, to be successful. I'd rather be an intern getting coffee."

"I'm sorry to hear that. I wished your showcase could've been all you had hoped."

"Me too, Lil. I still have my job, and I'll have another chance again, but I want it to be worth it."

"How do you mean?"

"I don't want to be doing anymore favors. I want to grow without having Giorgio and Martino supervising me and trying to make it seem like whatever they do for me is in our best interest."

"I want you to have that chance."

"I'm glad, Lil."

Lila felt as if Camille was smiling on the other side, and it made her smile.

"Do you have anymore questions for me?"

"Um, not really. If I have anymore, I'll let you know. Get some sleep."

"You always told me to sleep, even when we were on vacation."

Saturday morning found both Lila and Ben awake and enjoying breakfast with the traffic report as ambiance music. Lila sent pictures of her and Camille smiling in various tourist spots in Milan, and then was off work while Ben worked at the record store until three that afternoon, while dropping off his application to be a bartender at June Bug's Pub by noon. During their respective lunch hours, Lila and Ben drove out to Manhattan, arriving at Melville house. A certain man was especially happy to see her along with a former assistant.

"Well, hello stranger," Greta greeted as Lincoln gave Lila a welcoming hug.

"Did you leave him?" Lincoln asked, already knowing the answer. "Where are you working now?"

"You already know," giggled Lila.

"I told you that you working there wasn't too far fetched," responded Lincoln, his attention turning to Ben browsing. "Is he your boyfriend?"

Lila shook her head. "New roommate. Took him in, and he's looking for another job. Do you have a bartender's drink guide?"

"There's two different kinds," answered Greta. "I'll lead your roommate to them."

Greta left to assist leaving Lincoln and Lila to catch up on each other's lives. Lincoln became an uncle and accepted an intern from NYU while Lila became a "hotshot" travelling to one of the fashion epicenters for business and was able to obtain her bridesmaid's dress for Jay's wedding: a flowing mauve off-shoulder gown reaching just above her knees.

"Is Jay going to set you up with a groomsmen?" Lincoln asked.

"No, she knows I'm awkward at that stuff."

"You're able to speak with me."

Lila smirked. "Because you've seen me eat my weight in fried rice. There are no fronts I can use to keep that image away."

"Glad you got out of there."

"Speaking of, do you know how FTS is doing? Samson told me he dropped them as a client and sent them elsewhere," Lila pointed out.

"Foot in the Sand isn't around anymore," Lincoln answered to a shocked Lila. "The employees pretty much left after you did, and they didn't last long at Black Tar."

"What happened?"

Lila and Lincoln sat at a rest area with two couches and a floor lamp.

"From what a couple of the former employees told me, Walker tried to steal some of Black Tar's clients to seem more successful to other magazines and businesses and he tried to use his secretary to seal the deal with a few of them," Lincoln explained. "When she failed, he fired her."

Scarlett. "What happened to her?"

"She's trying to get into the modeling business; sending headshots and looking for an agent. Last I saw her, she's a cocktail waitress at a club on Broadway."

"Are any of the others better off?"

"Yes and no. Some were able to find work in better companies, and others are working slightly above entry level. I think one is the exception."

"Who?"

"One lady got a screenplay in circulation, and now she's getting recognition as a playwright. We help manage her."

"Tracy?"

"That's her." Lincoln smiled. "She says hi by the way. I assume you were close?"

Lila blushed. "Somewhat. What about Walker?"

"He came in about a week ago saying he lives in destitution, because of you. He's actually an English teacher at a private school in Queens."

"I hardly consider that destitution."

"You were too good for that place, and you should be glad about leaving them."

"I am."

By the early afternoon, Lila had to say goodbye to Lincoln and Greta. Ben was able to turn in his application and arrived early enough to seize an interview whereas Lila went back to Sal's to work on her article.

The fashion world is presented as glamorous and the place where millions of men and women flock to in order to get recognition of some kind. My sister, Camille, is among one of the millions who worked hard to make it where she is now. She spent a year learning Italian, went to one of the high-end fashion schools, and used that knowledge to secure a job where she earned gratitude from names people dream about seeing out on the street.

Entering Milan was leaving the big pond of New York and entering into an even bigger pond. The new pond felt comforting.

Seeing the simple and beautiful city subsides the part of yourself that tells you to not go certain places after dark. I only read about paradise, but I seldom experience it. The idea of paradise only continued when I arrived at my sister's. Fame treats her well, but she was modest about it.

Additionally, the city contrasted with the sister I thought I was familiar with and who grew up with me. Seeing my sister was as if time stood still. Camille was still beautiful, graceful, and feminine. Making it worse was how she seemed to not know it; despite the attention she regularly received from men and women. At first, I thought she was as fake as an airbrushed headshot, but she was genuine.

- *Insert notes about showcase*
  - *What she had to do to get it??*
  - *Past experience with what she had to do to advance in her job*
    - ASK WHAT I CAN AND CANNOT SAY
    - DON'T INCLUDE HER BEING A FAILURE
      - THROW AWAY NOTES FROM THE FIRST DAY!!!
- *Her dedication*
- *Memories making me see her as sympathetic*
- ***OUR LAST CONVERSATION***

Much like the designs and clothing presented in the fashion industry, only the best is shown (and known?) to the public. Designs and clothing are meant to make the model beautiful and disguise any supposed imperfections. Even the designs themselves start out as possibly imperfect concepts. It's all about building the right (?) connections to make it (different word?) presentable; the right designer, the right fabric, the right structure of the clothing, the right model, the right lightening, the right season. The list goes on.

IV

Beyond it All

After two large soda refills and three meatball subs, Lila exited Sal's. Driving back, she suddenly decided to make a detour to Queens. A quick search on Facebook brought Lila to St. Augustine's Academy for Young Ladies. School had let out, and girls in plaid skirts and knee high socks, black cardigans with their school's crest, and saddle shoes awaited rides from their parents and the bus. Lila drove around to the other side of the school, parking near the exit. Entering the school, Lila never felt so intimidated, and yet so scholarly. Her parents could have sent her and Camille to private school if they wanted to, but Lila was ultimately glad she wasn't. St. Augustine's entryway looked deep-rooted in secular beliefs, as there was something in Latin carved in. The only Latin Lila could remember was "tempus." Meanwhile, the inside of the school looked a bit more welcoming; mint green lockers, cream tiled floors that looked fairly clean, plaques and awards given by the school for excellence in academic standing and for certain well-achieving students, and portraits of the school's founders and benefactors. No women were presented.

Weaving her way between students staying for extracurriculars and a maze of hallways, Lila found a classroom with the name Johnson Walker on it. The door to the classroom was open. Inside the classroom were thirty desks lined up in straight rows of five, pictures of Hemingway, Dickens, Melville, and Tolstoy above a chalkboard, and a mahogany teacher's desk. Walker was behind that desk, and he didn't look too happy to see Lila.

"Have you come here to rub it in?"

Lila leaned on one of the students' desks. "What do you mean?"

"You're a big shot now, and I'm stuck babysitting girls who could care less about the symbolism of Vronsky's Racehorse."

"*Anna Karenina.*"

Walker smirked slightly. "You're too smart for your own good. No wonder you quit."

"You're lucky I quit. There was so much more I wanted to say to you, and so much more I could've used against you."

Walker's eyes widened.

Lila rose up from the desk. "You made me and Tracy give up our vacation days so you Scarlett could meet with that elusive 'Mr. Scotts' from Penguin. Not to mention keeping me from that travel writer position."

What's your point?

He's not even denying it. "Being mousy has its advantages. You shouldn't have made me a bookkeeper for the company. I could've given those records to the IRS, or publish them; they'd be best sellers. Could've used them, too. That was just the tip of the iceberg," Lila finished with a giggle.

Walker stood to face Lila. He didn't seem as tall as she remembered. "Why are you here? Trying to blackmail me? Get me fired again?"

Lila crossed her arms over her chest. "You're pathetic. Me leaving didn't make your life hell. *You* were the one sending offers to everyone else to keep me at bay. Seems like everyone is better off without you."

"Jolene is still with me."

Lila sighed. "I feel sorry for her."

"You don't even like her."

"Why does that matter? You made marriage trivial when you made your trips with Scarlett."

Walker attempted to remain stoic.

"You want me to leave, don't you?"

Walker nodded.

"Enjoy babysitting."

Immediately, Lila craved the four walls, kitchen, bathroom, and bedrooms of her apartment. Entering inside it brought Lila marginal comfort. There were the same pieces of furniture her parents got for her, some beginning to show their age. The large fabric sofa was softer on one side than the other. A violet throw blanket was draped over that side. There were the same Van Gogh and Monet prints of paintings on the walls of the living room and her bedroom Lila saw once gazed upon in museums. She wondered why she still kept them. Though an admirer of the artists, Lila considered owning their works to be predictable. It was an easy choice for a present her mom and dad to make during one of their outings. After spending ten minutes taking them down, Lila made it a point to find some Georgia O'Keefe prints, and something else Ben might like. It was his place, too, after all. To help him unwind, she called his favorite Chinese place for takeout to arrive when he got back from work. While she waited, she continued working on her article. Before she could edit her first paragraph, she got a call from her dad.

"Hi, is something wrong?" she asked, a bit surprised.

"Not really," Mr. Goods answered. "We're on our way to see Cammy, but she won't take any of our calls."

"Wait, what?" Lila asked, spitting out her sip of coffee.

"Your mother and I wanted to apologize to Cammy in person and take her out to wherever she wants, but she isn't answering her phone," explained Mr. Goods.

"One moment."

Lila sent a quick text message to Camille informing her that their dad was trying to get a hold of her. Camille's reply back was near instant.

I know. I'm busy. They'll understand.

Lila smiled internally. *She's starting to remember.* "She's swamped at work, but wants you and mom to enjoy your time exploring and playing tourist until she's done with work."

"Is she sure?" Mrs. Goods interjected, a slight scuffle for the phone occurring on the other line.

"She is."

"Alright. Tell her we love her and she's doing great."

"I will."

Lila hung up and returned to the article.

Aspiring writers I remember meeting want only their best to be viewed by the public. Fashion designers can say the same, except when they fail; their fall is more public on a global scale. (If anything,) writers are told privately by their publisher their doesn't meet their expectations and it stops there. Fashion designers will have some design rejected by an editor in chief, but when (those that) (design concepts) have been approved for the public are presented, the designer will know immediately what the reactions will be. That was the case of Camille's first solo exposé.

Her designs coming to life were extraordinary and beautiful (switch order) to a fashion-illiterate person such as myself, but to those who could name every shade of blue, they were unimpressive and too much like her mentors' work to be exclusively her own. She was told that she didn't have a voice in the fashion world. (?)

As a writer, one has to have a voice to stand out from the greats. The same goes for fashion; something I didn't think about. (Re-word?) Each designer label has some distinct feature (I think or assume), and writers have their own particular style. We are one in the same. My sister is right. I don't know everything. (Add later?) She puts herself through hell and back to get recognition for her work, and some of what she has done no one should do.

(Segway or transition somehow)

Detail her hard work

Use some of my memories of her working past midnight

Would that be too close to her secret??

Camille, though flighty at times, has a strong moral compass. Even when we were kids, she never ratted on me. Looking back, she was the one to encourage me to write more than our parents. I picture her graduating from fashion school and landing a job right away. Whether or not that was the case, she got the attention of world renounced fashion icons. To do this, she was coerced into chipping away at her moral compass. Her first instance was

Before Lila could finish the sentence, she texted Camille asking if she could use their conversation in her article in between calling Arthur.

"Yes, Lila?" Arthur asked.

"I have an conversation from my sister about her experiences in the fashion world, but some of it is a bit graphic. Do you want me to include it, or include the less graphic parts?" Lila requested.

A slight pause. "How graphic?" Arthur seemed concerned.

Lila looked around her apartment. Ben wasn't inside. "She's implied that her boss made her...um...prove her worth—"

"I get it. You can include it if you wish, but I want you to have your sister's permission. Secondly, if and when you get her permission, have it in writing and ask if she wishes to have her name and other names listed or changed."

"Already on it. Thank you."

"Good luck."

Her first instance was firing an employee my sister described as driven and passionate. The reason for this was allegedly to hire a busty blonde from a benefactor family. While the business of fashion is known for stunning women, it's more than almost-too skinny stoic-looking models strutting on a runway like (human?) (walking?) billboards (human NASCARs??). The most current injustice Camille had to endure was during my visit.

She came home late, and want to shuffle into her room had I not been waiting up for her. Right then, I was parent to my older sister. I guess it took her by surprise, but I'm guessing not by much considering how much we've depended on each other growing up as opposed to our parents. She even talked to me like a sitcom daughter would to her sitcom mother. Bob Saget, Florence Henderson, Alan Thicke, James Avery, and William Russ are among many other TV parents who raised us. (Move this sentence to the end. Use it more as a way to lead into an end?)

She poured her heart out to me, and seeing her like that made me want to guard Camille like a parent normally would.

A buzz on Lila's iPhone indicated an approval from Camille with an exception to not name her boss. Luckily for Lila, she didn't know who Camille's boss was. Not wanting to leave the apartment, she ordered a large meat lover's pizza and garlic bread. The food arrived a few minutes after Ben did, so neither of them had to cook anything. As Ben caught up on "Kitchen Nightmares", Lila continued her article until she received a phone call from her mom. It was the most she had ever heard from her in a short span of time.

"Is everything okay with Cammy?" she asked, no greeting or asking how Lila was doing.

"Yes. Why are you asking me?"

"She's barely picking up her phone. She sent us a few messages about being busy, even though your father and I have told her that we cleared our schedules for her. I admire her for working hard, but we're her parents after all. She should make time for the effort we're putting in."

"I know that." *Classic line.* "Just give her some space, Mom. Let her come to you. That's all I have right now. I have work I to do, so please figure these things out with Dad. You're the parents after all." Lila hung up and ignored the subsequent phone calls from her parents.

She poured her heart out to me, and seeing her like that made me want to guard Camille like a parent normally would. She confessed things (to me) no one should ever have to say. What stood out to me (the most) was her confession of (always) feeling inadequate to her "wise and gifted younger sister." Though Camille is passionate about her job, she shouldn't have come to the conclusion of trying to prove to our parents she was as good as me.

We lived a pretty upper class life; nothing was ever a problem for us. Financially. We had nice clothes, went to good schools, took vacations, had trust funds, and could go to school anywhere, but we never really had our mom and dad. Our vacations consisted of our parents being on assignment for National Geographic, and my sister and I being left to our own devices and often in the care of the hotel personnel. We both learned how to ask for our rooms, request room service, and ask what places were good to eat in in five languages when we reached our teens. A great thing to put on college applications and job résumés, according to our parents. That being said, maybe our parents are the reason my sister and I are recently trying to mend our bond. We had to parent each other and grow up relatively quickly. When I grew up faster than Camille, she took it as a sign of not growing up fast enough.

Note to self:
Switch order of the paragraphs
Think of other transition sentences

She tried on different personalities until one fit well enough to start her career (is this too on the nose??). She's stuck with that same personality to wear it was all I could see when I visited her. It wasn't until I went to her showcase when I saw beyond Camille's façade and saw her as my sister once again. As an expert in nipping and tucking, Camille did an excellent job in presenting herself in a certain light to everyone else in her circle. It took an outsider to navigate past the smoke and mirrors and peak behind the curtain. In more ways than one.

Camille is as imperfect and human as anyone else in the world, especially me. I'm glad I got to see her as my sister rather than the favorite child. Truth of the matter is, I don't think any one of us was the Favorite. We both got some attention and some praise for our abilities and talents, but neither one of us felt as valuable to them as their work. We had to figure out our own value. I don't know if either one of us have completely figured it out yet or I don't know how long it will take.

Maybe this will be the first step. Our mutual understanding (?) will come to us, and when it does, I'll be there to greet my sister without any of our memories altering the way I see her. Not again.

Is it a good end??

It was five in the morning when Lila painstakingly arose from her desk to shuffle into the kitchen to make a pot of her beloved caffeinated elixir. She sent her newest article to Arthur after taking into account the notes she made for herself. By six-thirty, Lila had a staple breakfast of eggs and sausage patties before showering and dressing for work. The moment she sat in her desk, Arthur called her into his office.

"Yes, sir?" Lila asked after sitting down.

"I read your latest article, and I prefer it over the first one," Arthur said. "The board wants to use the first one." Arthur sat at his desk to face Lila, "but I know you don't want that."

"Why not?"

"Your revised draft comes across as more personal and multi-dimensional. It interweaves your experiences with your sister with both of your careers in a way I never realized. You're both passionate, but your new one seems to have a purpose. Not to just make amends with your sister, but to make amends with yourself and the life you two were dealt." His voice was still soft, yet still commanding a presence.

My hard work is being reduced to spite. "What's going to happen?" Lila felt a bead of sweat run down her neck.

Arthur's tone became softer. He almost sounded like Lincoln. "I don't know. I'll hear back from corporate later today about what the final decision will be, and inform you about it, but please know that I personally don't want your original piece published."

"If only corporate saw my article the way you do."

"Give them time."

Arthur stood up from his desk, mentally exhausted, leaving his office to attend to some pressing matter. Lila returned to her desk, answering phone calls and scheduling upcoming appointments with writers.

Before the day was over, she had to scan the approved articles for Arthur to send to corporate via the Cloud. She scanned them blankly, sending them to Arthur, who would be staying in the office late.

When the finally workday ended, Lila was pleased to find no more calls from her parents and to find Ben laid out on the sofa studying from "Bartending for Dummies"; one of the few times Ben was around during the afternoon, but most likely not going to be around much longer.

Luckily, Ben needed Lila to practice mixing drinks with. After three failed tequila sunrises and two successful Manhattans, Lila felt the urge to open up to the soon-to-be barkeep.

"I'm partially screwed at work."

Ben rolled his eyes, but played along with the trope. "What's eating you?"

"I write this piece about my sister and her job in spite and send it. Then we have a heart-to-heart after, and write a new piece—"

"And your boss favors the other?"

"Corporate does, but they don't know about my other one. My boss wants to keep my new article, but part of me doubts how far he'll go to defend it."

"Why?" Ben absent-mindedly cleaned the kitchen counter with a rag.

"I haven't had the best experience with 'Give me time' or 'Give it time.' How will I know if my boss will fight for me while maintaining his professional image?"

Ben chuckled. "Never known you to ask others to fight for you."

"My hands are tied!"

"Does she know that already?"

"I would hope so. I told her I was going to rewrite the article."

"Maybe show it to her." Ben took away Lila's half-empty Manhattan.

"It won't be published until a couple weeks after my boss accepts it, and it may not even be the one we both want."

Ben rolled his eyes again. "I repeat: maybe show it to her." He poured her a mint julep, then prepared to leave for work.

Lila took out her phone and her computer. Arthur informed her that corporate decided to publish the first draft. Lila decided to take some action.

Hey, Camille. I think my boss is going to print out the first article I sent. In preparation, I'm sending you the one I wanted to take its place with. Don't be mad at me. —L

She sent the text in addition to an email with the article attached. She wouldn't hear back from Camille for a week.

"I want to do right by Camille."

When the two sisters finally conversed, no harsh words or pleasantries were exchanged. The two sisters caught up and made arrangements to meet for the upcoming Easter. Lila wanted to know what Camille thought of the revised article, but she felt as if there wasn't a chance considering how brief Camille was keeping their conversation.

"Do you think you did the right thing?" Ben asked as Lila was heading to a work dinner.

Lila nodded quickly before heading out to meet with her co-workers at Patsy's Italian Restaurant. There was standard chitchat and sharing of not-too-personal personal anecdotes from the Sterling employees. No one ordered too many drinks or anything too expensive as everyone received separate checks in the end. After the Human Resources manager oversaw the collective tip, each person parted ways until they would meet again on next workday.

Before Lila could completely settle in, Arthur called her into his office again. His tone was urgent and grave.

"We have a problem," Arthur stated, motioning Lila to sit down, but she was too on edge to sit still. "Corporate is coming here in *ten minutes*," rambled Arthur, raking his fingers through his hair nervously. "This isn't good."

"What happened?" Lila watched Arthur pace around his desk, his eyes darting in every direction.

"Corporate realized the wrong article got published, and it's too late to recall the magazine," Arthur explained, his hands trembling slightly, "and now someone's job is on the line!"

"My job?"

"And mine!"

Lila was stunned. "What did you do?"

"I sent in your revised article. I was working late, and I had your revised one on my file. I mixed them up when approving them for the Cloud. By accident, I swear."

Lila wasn't convinced. She would have been touched about Arthur doing that for her if he didn't look so apprehensive.

"What am I going to do?"

Lila approached her boss slowly. "If things look bleak, I'll put in my three weeks notice—"

"What are you—"

"I'm not going to be responsible for you losing your job. You compromised your professional integrity, because of me. If I stay, you'll probably be reminded of it." Lila's heart was palpating, but she remained firm.

"You're not going to sacrifice yourself, Lila!"

"I'll only do it if there's no way out. Your job means more to Sterling than mine."

Arthur wanted to further protest against Lila's drastic and rash decision, but with more pressing matters at hand, he had to think of a strategy of how to avoid unnecessary losses when whomever from corporate would come; fully prepared with intimidating and piercing statements and declarations.

Lila returned to the apartment, immediately going to her refrigerator. She found a roll of chocolate chip cookie dough, peeled back the plastic wrap, and alleviated her stress. Later, Lila barricaded herself in her room and put her phone on silent. She needed her thoughts to tell her what to do. She had to get serious once again, even more so than she had in her lifetime.

No more rash moments.

"Dare I ask what happened?" Ben asked, seeing Lila and half the roll of cookie dough in her hand.

"My boss defied the superiors," Lila answered.

"Is that a good thing or a bad thing?"

Lila clenched the tube of cookie dough tighter. "My job, along with my boss's, is on the line."

Ben rose from his seat. "What happened?"

Lila gave Ben a brief, yet informative answer to her and Arthur's crisis. Though Lila expected Ben to be worried for her and her boss, he seemed pensive and deep in thought, analyzing Arthur's motives behind his so-called last minute decision; something Lila overlooked.

"What do you know about him?" Ben asked after a ten-minute silence.

"He's an incredibly professional man. He maintains non-personal relationships with his co-workers, but remains cordial with them. He seems like the type to sign his name on a birthday card, but not include a super sentimental note in it."

Ben took mental notes. "How is he with you?"

"Better than my first boss. He listens to me, seems to think I'm valuable to the company, and gets offended if I dare eat anything from the bottom of my purse or the microwave."

"What else makes him a good boss?"

"He calls me by my first name."

Ben pondered Lila's last comment for a moment.

"Has Arthur had other people work for him before you?"

Lila looked surprised. "I would assume so."

"Do you know how his relationships were with them?"

"Probably the same as it is with me."

"What happened to them? Do you know if they quit or were fired?"

"I don't know."

"Then you might want to ask your boss about it."

"He'd never tell me about them."

"Find a way to weave it into your conversation. He might reveal something, even if it may seem like nothing."

"How do I do that?"

"It's up to you."

Barely a month passed before Lila had the time ask Arthur Samson about his choice. In between scheduling 5:00 pm Friday calls with Camille, 6:00 pm text updates from her parents, setting up an OkCupid account, and attending Jay's small, intimate wedding at her family's summer home with a newly legal drinking-aged Ben as her plus-one, Lila found herself writing more poetry and short stories to send to independent literary magazines. Lila's favorite memory of the wedding was how the couple each wore blue Converse during the ceremony. She even wrote a poem for Jay's wedding affectionately titled "Blue Feet".

While both Arthur and Lila's jobs remained reasonably in tact, their conversations had become shorter and sporadic. There had even been moments where Arthur would spend his workday locked away in his office only to come out for bathroom breaks and staff lunches.

After a staff lunch, Lila sprung the question "Why did you choose the other article instead?" on Arthur.

"In my office" was the prelude to a complex answer.

"More people can relate to a voice investigating why one is frustrated, confused, and eventually peaceful in their lives. I never had a sibling, but the revised article made me feel something. It made me feel angry, but it sent the message that not everything can be wrapped up nicely in a pretty bow. Dreams, specifically your sister's, don't always equate to a happy ending.

"In movies and TV shows, everything is settled in twenty minutes or less. That does not reflect real life. I want our readers to know more about it, and make them think. Anger makes no one think, and turns them into the most honest and hurtful versions of themselves. While you keep some of your anger in your piece, I was glad to see it not cloud your judgment. You use it to find answers you probably will be looking for for the rest of your life. It makes you so much smarter than those at corporate. All they seem to want are fast sales and no lasting impressions. Tell no one I said that."

Lila was delighted. "What made you think that I can make a lasting impression?"

"You did with me."

"How?"

"If you remember, I wasn't exactly polite to you. You kept a level head and put me in my place. It's not everyday where someone impresses me after one meeting. It's also not everyday where I take that someone in immediately. Though part of the reason was your past experience at FTS, the main one was because you have the experience to be a journalist *and* head editor. Whatever you do here has the potential to be great. I want corporate to remember you for more than fifteen minutes."

A content "Thank you" was the last exchange between the two. Lila returned to her desk to check up on the progress of Sterling's writers as Arthur's attention went back to his tedious paperwork.

It was six-thirty when Lila returned to the apartment to Ben taking notes from two books: a bartending manual and a psychology book.

"Is that why you were interviewing me?" Lila probed, indicating the textbook.

Ben nodded. "Practicing for when I go into criminal justice." He closed his books, went to the fridge for leftover spaghetti and meatballs, and began eating it cold. "Enrolled in Hostos Community College while you were on vacation. Professor's cool, I guess."

"Was I a guinea pig?" Lila joked, pulling out another container of leftover pasta, taking the extra step to heat it up in a pan.

"More or less," Ben answered with a stuffed mouth.

Lila stifled a smile as she joined Ben on the sofa. The two stared blankly at the reporters on CNN. Pulling Lila away from the television was a call from Camille.

"Is something wrong?"

"I just wanted to say thank you." Camille seemed touched that Lila was concerned about her. "The article you wrote about me got me a promotion and I have a secretary now."

"That's great. What else happened?"

"Jerome and I might get serious again, but we still have to deal with the others."

The Armani Men. "Why? Wouldn't a promotion get you closer from getting away from them?"

"No. They're the heads of the company and they oversee everything. Unless I quit and move to another company, they're always going to be my bosses."

"Do that!"

"I can't." Camille's tone was dry. "I don't want to do anything else other than be a fashion designer. It's too late for me to change my career."

"But—"

Camille became eager and joyful again, much to Lila's dismay. "I'm glad we get meet for Easter. I'll take you to the Vatican. Bring a nice dress and shoes."

Lila sighed. "I will."

There was a note on Lila's desk from Arthur: "My office. 10 AM. CRITICAL." Lila confirmed three appointments for the week while reviewing the latest bestsellers lists to occupy her thoughts. Once it reached the foreseen 10:00 AM, Lila walked into Arthur's office.

"Are you alright?"

Lila shook her head. "I'm so excited…I'm so excited."

"Eighties or nineties?"

"Nineties. *'Saved By the Bell.'* Jessie gets addicted to caffeine pills to stay awake to study, because Zach manipulates her to be a singer and causes her to break down."

"Good to know. Share an elevator with me?"

"Yes."

It was just the two of them inside the elevator. Arthur was the one who pushed for the top floor, as Lila's palms were sweaty.

"Am I going to lose my job?" Lila asked.

"Hopefully not. Who else can recite lines from 'Full House' to me verbatim?"

Lila placed her hands on her hips. "So that's all I'm good at?"

"At least I'm catching up on sitcoms so I can at least learn some comebacks."

"You can learn those anywhere." Lila took a deep breath. "What should I expect from corporate?"

"Honestly, anything, but don't take their first offer."

Inside the spacious office were wall-to-wall windows on one side of the office, a decorative plant and wireless projector on the other, and a large, narrow mahogany table with four intimidating-looking men ranging from early thirties to middle-aged in tailored suits on each side and one at the front. All of them turned to face Arthur and Lila when they were permitted to enter. A man mirroring Christian Bale from "American Psycho" stood up to address the two. "Mr. Samson. Ms. Goods. Glad you made it on time." His voice was like that of a Bond villain: calculating and suave.

"Let me first say that what was done was a breech of professional integrity," the man continued, walking around the desk to personally address Arthur. The two men were about the same height, but the man from corporate projected his seniority over Arthur. "It is so unlike you to defy your superiors. Shame."

"Yes, Sir."

The man turned to Lila.

"The wordsmith, I presume?"

"Yes, Sir," responded Lila.

"You're not what I expected." He scanned Lila slowly. "You sound older in your articles."

"Is that all you wish to tell me?"

The man was taken aback. Three of the other men in the room looked back at each other, mumbling to each other. One of them stifled a smirk. Arthur seemed to be one the only one who smiled at Lila's assertiveness.

"Since your assistant is dead-set on bringing this meeting to a start, I'll show you why we've called you here," replied the man, using a sleek-looking remote to turn on the projector. "What you see here is our sales of articles in our fiction and journalism during the past month." A laser pointer indicated a bar graph display—one blue and one red. "As of right now, we have experienced a rising sale in our journalism field by nearly forty percent." He indicated a red bar noticeably taller than the blue one.

"That's wonderful, Mr. Lucas," responded Arthur coolly.

"Quite right, Mr. Samson," Mr. Lucas agreed. "You should be proud of your assistant."

"I am, but she's my commissioning editor."

"Not for long," Mr. Lucas retorted, putting Lila and Arthur on edge.

"Am I fired?" choked Lila.

"Of course not." Mr. Lucas's attention was on Lila. "I and the rest of your superiors are going to start a new division of Sterling, and we've appointed you and Mr. Samson to be the heads of it."

Lila was speechless. Her dream was coming true.

"Heads of what division?" Arthur interjected.

"One of us was thinking of an advice column, but we've come to the consensus of employing the both of you as travel writers," Mr. Lucas concluded.

"In fact, we have an assignment for you," another man interjected. "There's a new pop singer making waves in Rio. We want to know more about her, specifically about her allegedly running away from home to pursue her career."

"Um, sounds interesting, but—" Lila started, only for Arthur to stop her.

"It seems like a piece a woman's magazine would do. Lila and I want something more serious. You've seen what she's capable of."

"Yes, but if Lila were to take on this assignment, we will sweep the previous mess under the rug," Mr. Lucas challenged.

"You're blackmailing Lila?" Arthur gasped.

"Of course not," retorted Mr. Lucas. "We all agreed that the little SNAFU would be disregarded no matter what. With that in mind, business is business and your employer has been given an assignment each and every one of us highly recommend she take." He turned to Lila. "What do you think, dear?"

"I'll need to think about what kind of angle to take," Lila responded. "Do you want me to use a certain stance? Do you want me to take a side?"

"We trust your judgment. Thank you both for your time," Mr. Lucas concluded.

Arthur and Lila said their cordial goodbyes, leaving the corporate office. In the privacy of an elevator, Arthur decided to voice his concerns.

"What were you thinking about taking that assignment? It's something you see splashed in between *Cosmo* ads just to make it sound respectable!"

"I'm not learning about who she's dating and if she's taking part in a dangerous fad diet," returned Lila. "I want to know her story."

"Running away, because her parents were too strict and that they 'just didn't understand her' and forced her in some sort of a metaphorical box?"

"Are you done, Mr. Belding?"

"Now she's some a wild child who 'doesn't know how to stop?'" Arthur regained his more level tone. "Okay. Now, I'm done."

"We don't know that. Maybe she had a good reason for leaving."

"So me forbidding you won't work?" Arthur sighed, defeated after he and Lila exited the elevator.

"Why deny yourself a paid vacation?"

"Fine, but I'm going to complain the whole time."

"Brush up on your Spanish. I'll have someone to tell me what my curfew is."

"You're never going to let this go, are you?"

Lila shook her head. "May I go back to work now?"

Afterword

As someone growing up during times when both parents worked and I was left home alone, I would watch a variety of sitcoms until my mom would come home and ask if I had done my homework. Once my dad found more stable work, we found TV shows to watch together, usually "Everybody Loves Raymond" and some of the older Disney channel shows. From these shows, I assembled certain tropes commonly used: traditional family dynamics, often-toxic relationships with in-laws, fathers who were either oblivious or over-bearing for comedic effect, and the brunt of how well the kid or kids turned out was based on one parent, specifically the mother. The older I got, the more I realized how those tropes I used to find amusing could be harmful.

Behind the scenes, most of the sitcom actors try to escape their legacies of studio audiences and laugh tracks. In most cases, their lives become static and the adjustment from one role to another can be a shock. This may or may not be known to those who grew up watching sitcom actors. Given this, my goal was to show how much of life, specifically my life in a few years, might turn out in contrast to the formula of family and teen sitcoms. I wanted to stick with realistic situations characters would and could face–a constant feeling of not belonging even when one does, and having a band of strong supporting characters that help the protagonist forward. For most of my adolescent life, I felt as if I didn't entirely belong. Right way, I was marked as someone new and different. I wasn't in tuned with inside jokes and deep bonds my friends' friends had. To find a place where I could fit in, or forget my troubles, I turned to television.

Re-runs of "Everybody Loves Raymond" played from 3-4pm. I would sit in the living room with a snack, watch the episodes, do my homework in between commercials, and wait for my parents to come home. Saturday mornings were for "Full House" and "Saved by the Bell." One thing I was fasci- nated by was how much one person could do wrong, and yet in half an hour everything was forgiven and forgotten in the next episode and/or season. Real life didn't work like that. I never want to blindly forgive someone who turns a cold shoulder on me for protecting them from those who might want to harm them, and if it loses me friends, then it's ultimately their decision.

I could come up with a million and one ideas for sto- ries, but translating them onto paper is an entirely different matter. I had to get my ideas on paper, and they had to be as close to perfect as I could manage. I've done works before, but only was this was going to be a reflection of me. As a writer, I already know the first draft of something will not be perfect. By extension, I'm far from a perfect writer. With that, I can reach out to other writers and those I feel close enough to share my work with so they can bring out the writer they see in me and the writer I know I can be. Only somewhat recently have I made some of my work public, but a majority of them had been private. Having to make my work so public was something I wish I knew ahead of time; I would've been a bit more particular with my words and more selective with some of the ideas I wanted to use. However, sending my work in the earliest stages to be edited and looked over was helpful. I could better decide what to keep and what to cut. I won't be so shy as to do it continually, depending on what the subject of my work will be.

In the young adult books I have read, there is a lack of treating some serious issues and characters with varying personalities. Characters are either hated or made to be so faultless to where they are Mary Sue-types. I believe characters should break away from commonplace archetypes. They may not break away entirely, but it would be a welcome edition to make the archetypes more relatable rather than having their entire personality be one thing. Just because one person is the "nice guy", doesn't mean that deep down they're imperfect. And because they're imperfect, it doesn't mean they should automatically be pitied. People by nature are not perfect, and are not limited to one personality and one identity. Similarly, there isn't just one way to handle a situation. Lila dives into academics to set herself up for success, but is reliant on clichéd plot points and hammy morals to grow up mentally and emotionally. It's when she meets up with her sister again that she can break away from overused tropes to build a more realistic and sobering relationship with her sister.

From this, I want to write books young adults and older adults can identify with; feeling lost, trying to find their place in a world, and wanting their lives have meaning. They want to be involved in causes and make a difference, but want their own voices to be heard. Maybe I can be a voice, not *the* voice, but a voice that acknowledges their insecurities and listens.

Acknowledgements

Thank you to all of my family; formed by blood, the heart, late nights with caffeinated drinks, and procrastinating afternoons by the television.

For,
Devin
Mom
Papa
Wella

About the Author

Idalis is a graduate student of Linfield College with a degree in Creative Writing. Her dream is to become a novelist and/or poet. As an aspiring writer, Idalis hope my words can inspire and make a difference in the lives of others. Since the age of ten, Idalis has always wanted to write stories. Eventually it turned to writing books.

During her time as a writer, she has published a handful of short stories and poems in magazines such as her alma mater's magazine Camas, Underscore Review, The Paragon Press, Shift: A Journal of Literary Oddities, and even Adelaide Literary Magazine. In addition to writing stories and poems, Idalis has dabbled in writing plays and while in college, took a course in screenplay writing. Whatever she can write, she dabbles in, but her preferences are fiction and poetry.

Idalis is currently married living in Oregon with her husband Devin, who is often the first to hear any news about her writing submissions.